Summer Escapes

Can you take the heat?

Love is in the air and the forecasts have promised a spell of sun, sea and sizzling romance. So let us whisk you away to this season's most glamorous destinations full of rolling hills, blissful beaches and piping hot passion! Take your seat and follow as these sun-kissed couples find their forever on faraway shores. After all, it's been said you should catch flights, not feelings—but who says you can't do both?

Start your journey to true love in...

The Venice Reunion Arrangement
by Michelle Douglas

Dating Game with Her Enemy
by Justine Lewis

The Billionaire She Loves to Hate
by Scarlett Clarke

Cinderella's Greek Island Temptation
by Cara Colter

A Reunion in Tuscany
by Sophie Pembroke

Their Mauritius Wedding Ruse
by Nina Milne

Available now!

And look out for the next stop of your travels with...

Fake Date on the Orient Express
by Jessica Gilmore

Coming soon!

Dear Reader,

As I started writing their story, it was clear to me that both Logan and Chloe like to be in control of their destiny. They both decided categorically that love is not for them, that their pasts dictate they don't deserve love. So when they meet each other, the only way they can deal with the growing emotions is to try to control them...as if it's possible to shut love down. For a while I wasn't sure they wouldn't succeed—I hope you enjoy reading how they learned that love was something they couldn't control.

Nina x

THEIR MAURITIUS WEDDING RUSE

NINA MILNE

ROMANCE

If you purchased this book without a cover you should be aware that this book is stolen property. It was reported as "unsold and destroyed" to the publisher, and neither the author nor the publisher has received any payment for this "stripped book."

ISBN-13: 978-1-335-21647-2

Their Mauritius Wedding Ruse

Copyright © 2025 by Nina Milne

All rights reserved. No part of this book may be used or reproduced in any manner whatsoever without written permission.

Without limiting the author's and publisher's exclusive rights, any unauthorized use of this publication to train generative artificial intelligence (AI) technologies is expressly prohibited.

This is a work of fiction. Names, characters, places and incidents are either the product of the author's imagination or are used fictitiously. Any resemblance to actual persons, living or dead, businesses, companies, events or locales is entirely coincidental.

For questions and comments about the quality of this book, please contact us at CustomerService@Harlequin.com.

TM and ® are trademarks of Harlequin Enterprises ULC.

Harlequin Enterprises ULC
22 Adelaide St. West, 41st Floor
Toronto, Ontario M5H 4E3, Canada
www.Harlequin.com

Printed in U.S.A.

Nina Milne has always dreamed of writing for Harlequin Romance—ever since she played libraries with her mother's stacks of Harlequin romances as a child. On her way to this dream, Nina acquired an English degree, a hero of her own, three gorgeous children and—somehow!—an accountancy qualification. She lives in Brighton and has filled her house with stacks of books—her very own *real* library.

Books by Nina Milne

Harlequin Romance

Royal Sarala Weddings

His Princess on Paper
Bound by Their Royal Baby

The Casseveti Inheritance

Italian Escape with the CEO
Whisked Away by the Italian Tycoon
The Secret Casseveti Baby

The Christmas Pact

Snowbound Reunion in Japan

Winter Escapes

Cinderella's Moroccan Midnight Kiss

Falling for His Stand-In Fiancée
Consequence of Their Dubai Night
Wedding Planner's Deal with the CEO

Visit the Author Profile page
at Harlequin.com for more titles.

To my lovely husband for listening to me.

Praise for
Nina Milne

"*Their Christmas Royal Wedding* is an escapist,
enjoyable and emotional contemporary tale that
will touch readers' hearts with its beguiling blend of
searing intensity, heart-warming drama and uplifting
romance. Nina Milne writes with plenty of warmth
and heart and she has penned a poignant and
spellbinding romantic read."
—*Goodreads*

CHAPTER ONE

LOGAN JAMIESON WALKED towards yet another swish, corporate building housing yet another top-notch firm of London solicitors. It was his third such visit of the day and, just as on his two previous visits, he wished with all his heart that he was going somewhere else, anywhere else. To work, where he played the stock markets, building wealth portfolios and adding millions to the billion he already had in the bank. Or to the beach to surf, walk or cycle. Or out for dinner with a beautiful woman...

No, better yet, out for dinner with his grandmother who, come to that, was still a beautiful woman. At eighty-three, Belle Jamieson still had what it took; her classic bone structure combined with impeccable taste and fashion sense made sure of that.

But now Logan wasn't sure how many

more dinners there would be. His chest tightened as he recalled the diagnosis, backed up by the second and third opinions he'd insisted on. His grandmother, his indomitable grandmother—the woman who had effectively brought him up with minimum, part-time input from his father, whilst founding a global cosmetic business she still ran—had suffered a heart attack.

Investigations had subsequently shown it had been more serious than 'just' a heart attack. He'd thought a heart attack was bad enough. But Belle Jamieson had cardiomyopathy and it was advanced. Yes, they could operate, but heart surgery on an eighty-three-year-old was risky, however tough she was.

Regret, guilt and a whole other plethora of emotions had run their gamut within him since the heart attack and coalesced into a wish that he'd been there more for Belle in recent years. They were close, and Logan would never forget what he owed his grandmother but, in the past five years since he'd made his first million, he had spent more time away from London than in it. Had bought a place in Sydney, one in California and another in Scotland.

He had created distance because in some ways it was easier for both of them. Because, whilst Belle claimed she understood why Logan refused to get involved in the running of her company, her pride and joy, Logan knew she was disappointed with that decision. He had believed—hoped—that the distance would help. Now it didn't feel that way; now it felt as though somehow this was on him. The idea caused a bitter taste in his mouth and crystallised a determination that he would make things right.

In a small way, that was why Logan was here. His grandmother had instructed him to find a solicitor. She wanted a fresh pair of eyes, a new voice with which to discuss her affairs. The doctors had advised rest and recuperation to build her strength, but Belle had been insistent, and Logan believed that thwarting her would make things worse, not better.

Especially as he understood how Belle must be feeling. He knew his grandmother was chafing at the impact of the heart attack on her company, worried about what would happen to it whilst she wasn't at the helm. Now she must be trying to work out how to preserve her legacy if the unthinkable happened and the operation resulted in her death.

How to preserve the global empire she'd built from nothing? A cosmetics brand that combined exclusivity with the high street, 'Belle's' products could be found everywhere. And she was still running the business herself. There was that nagging voice of guilt again, but he'd told himself it was because it was what Belle wanted to do: she'd always said nothing would drag her away from the helm. But perhaps that was because there was no successor to take over the family business. Maybe she would have pulled back if Logan had fulfilled her wishes.

Logan pushed the thought away. Now was not the time to rake over the tragically complicated Jamieson family history, the complexities, doubts, grief, anger and guilt that compounded the relationships between Matt and Belle and between Matt and Logan. Now wasn't the time to dwell on the fact that Logan couldn't get hold of his father and that Matt didn't know of Belle's heart attack because he'd done one of his disappearing acts and was non-contactable, off on his travels somewhere.

Logan hadn't seen his father in six years, but occasionally Matt sent a text or a postcard and Logan had always assumed he would be able to get hold of him in an emergency. Turned out it wasn't so simple. But that wasn't a problem for this minute.

Right now, Logan needed to walk through the revolving glass door, approach the reception desk and announce his arrival.

'I'll let Chloe know you're here,' the receptionist said.

Logan offered up a silent hope that this time he'd hit the jackpot. His previous two interviews had not been a success. Perhaps he'd been too harsh, but he wouldn't let either of the candidates anywhere near his grandmother or her business. Both of them had blatantly been too ambitious, too eager to impress him with how they knew all about business law and how they could manipulate and create corporate loopholes. Both had been happy to bad-mouth their rivals, both too arrogant and too sure of themselves.

Though perhaps Logan was being too protective, he was looking for the best. Maybe it was too much to hope that the best could also be likeable.

The lift doors swished open, a woman headed towards him. Logan sensed his jaw drop open, quickly snapped it shut and told himself to pull himself together before he made a fool of himself by forgetting his name. Or, worse, forgetting why he was here.

Yet, despite the reminder, it was impossible to ignore his body's reaction to the woman walking towards him. Impossible not to notice the glorious colour of her hair, a shade of strawberry-blonde that captured motes of red and gold, pulled back but allowing a few stray tendrils to frame features of classical beauty. She had high, slanted cheek bones, a straight nose and hazel eyes fringed by long lashes.

Damn it, he was still staring, and he saw a quizzical look in her eyes as she said, or possibly repeated, 'Logan Jamieson?'

'Yes. Yes. That's me.' He scrambled his brain back together. 'You must be Chloe Edwards. It's good to meet you.'

'Likewise.'

Logan looked down at her outstretched hand, aware of a strange reluctance to take it combined with a ridiculous urge to keep looking at it. The fingers were long and slender, her wrist encircled by a delicate silver chain.

He shook her hand and, as his fingers clasped hers, a jolt of desire clenched his gut, so sudden, so visceral, that he dropped her hand as though scorched.

And now her eyes were no longer quizzical; instead they were wide, first with an answering awareness that tinged her cheeks with heat and then with a surprise that mirrored his own. Though, she was the first to recover, managing a cool smile as she turned and gestured.

'Please come this way, Mr Jamieson.' The formality was perhaps designed to underscore that whatever had just happened was not to be acknowledged, a sentiment he completely agreed with—he had no intention of letting attraction bias his judgement. In any case, he had too much on his plate right now to be distracted, or rather blindsided, by an attraction. Dating was the very last thing on his mind.

He followed her down a corridor to a light, airy meeting room.

'Would you like coffee or tea?' she asked.

'No, thank you. I'm good.'

'Then let's get down to business.'

Business, Chloe repeated to herself. Though, truth to tell—and it wasn't a truth she much

14   THEIR MAURITIUS WEDDING RUSE

liked—for once in her work-focused, career-oriented life she was looking at a client and it wasn't only business that sprung to mind. Which was…ridiculous, unexpected, and she needed to close it down.

It didn't matter that Logan Jamieson was undoubtedly easy on the eye, with blond hair a touch over-long and spiky, dark-brown eyes that held a gleam she couldn't quite interpret and a firm jaw that spoke of character.

Not that Chloe had been able to discover much about his actual character. As she always did with any prospective client, she had done her research on Logan Jamieson, but to little avail; he was a resolutely private man. A billionaire in his own right who liked to remain under the radar, his wealth derived from his wealth-management company. It was an entirely separate entity from Belle's, the cosmetic company his grandmother had founded. As for his personal life, she had found virtually nothing but a scant fact here and there: his age, twenty-seven; his status, a bachelor.

But today Logan was here as his grandmother's representative and Chloe knew she was one of three candidates he was considering. Winning a client of Belle Jamieson's prestige would be more than a feather in her cap—it would be a whole designer hat of feathers and would take her another rung up the ladder to partnership.

Which made it imperative she didn't screw this up. Especially not over a pair of brown eyes, a body of sculpted muscle and a hand shake that had sent skitters of desire through her. She had to be on her game and not distracted by the man now sitting opposite her.

It was unfortunate that said man chose that moment to smile and, despite herself, she blinked, literally dazzled by the warmth, the crinkle of his eyes and the way his face creased. *Good Lord.* She had to get a grip.

Realising she was actually gripping the edge of the table, she forced herself to relax. Reminded herself that, when this meeting was over, she had a meeting scheduled with a senior partner and she wanted to have something positive to report, other than, *Well, Lou, the man was hot.* Somehow, she didn't think that was going to cut it.

Aware that the silence had gone a beat too long, aware too of something she couldn't quite define in the air, Chloe forced her lips upward into a professional, cool, *competent* smile.

'So, to business. I am obviously pleased that you are considering me as an advisor to your grandmother. I assume you have some questions you want to put to me, and I hope you are going to tell me a bit more about how I can be of help if chosen.'

'In brief, following her recent heart attack, my grandmother wants a fresh pair of eyes to look over some of her business interests and advise her. That's all I know.'

Chloe saw the shadow that crossed his eyes when he spoke of his grandmother's health, and her next words were instinctive. 'I was truly sorry to hear of the heart attack. I realise this sounds a little cheesy, but your grandmother is an inspiration—to me and a lot of other women looking to break glass ceilings. She made a difference. I hope and wish her a full recovery.'

The words were no more than the absolute truth. Even as a teenager, she had been inspired by Belle Jamieson and how she had set up her own company in her forties, had made it an overnight success then grown it to global proportions. Also by the way she spoke of parity for women in the workplace, and how she pioneered products aimed at women of all ages, as well as men. It had made the younger Chloe want to make a difference too.

But not as a corporate lawyer. That had been her brother's dream. The irony unbearable because Chloe *had* made a difference, but not for good. She'd screwed up, and her father and brother had paid the ultimate price. Their deaths were on her. Her fault. A fact she knew with bone-deep knowledge.

For a moment she was fifteen years old again, numbed by the news of the accident that had killed her father and brother. Was walking towards her mother, wanting to give and receive comfort, but stopped short by the blaze of her mother's eyes.

'This is your fault, Chloe. Yours. You caused this.' The words had been clear and sharp in the air—razor-blade sharp. 'Don't come near me. This is your fault. They wouldn't have been in that car if it wasn't for you. If you hadn't lied and deceived us.'

The words had stunned her, stopped her in her tracks as she'd realised the truth of them, the irrefutable, irrevocable awful truth of them. A truth that was etched on her very soul. And, God knew, if she could have turned back the clock, she would have sold that soul to do so.

But she couldn't. She had lied in order to go to a party with a boyfriend her parents had forbidden her to see. Then, when it had become too much, she'd called her dad to get her, and of course he had agreed. He'd brought James with him but they'd never made it. Instead they'd crashed. Because of her.

Now she was trying to win some sort of salvation by living her brother's dream for him. Salvation, and perhaps some forgiveness from her mother. She'd worked it out when she'd been sixteen, when she'd been studying for her exams. Her mother had said how the world had lost so much; that James would have achieved so much if he could have fulfilled his dreams. So Chloe had decided she would fulfil her brother's plans, thinking maybe that would bring some balm to her mother's grief and to the wrenching, searing guilt Chloe lived with every day.

It was a plan that gave her purpose and, most importantly, it brought some measure of happiness to her mother. In the ten years since, the only times Chloe had felt any sense of bond with her mother was when she had shared a step that followed in James's footprints.

If she pulled this off, won another promotion, perhaps that would bring a smile of pride to her mother's face. Be a small step closer to redemption. Even if she knew nothing could really redeem her in her mother's eyes, or her own.

Enough. She focused on Logan's voice.

'Thank you. My grandmother has always wanted to make a difference. She tried to run her company as ethically and fairly as possible. She believes in equality, but she also won't hire a woman solely because she is a woman.'

'And that's how it should be. I don't want this job because of my gender. I want it if I would be the best person for it.'

'If?' he asked and she met his gaze straight on, seeing the surprise there.

'Yes.' She eyed him thoughtfully, trying not to let her gaze linger over-long on his lips, the jut of his jaw. *'If.* You are here to work out if I am the best person for the job. Now, obviously I can reel off my qualifications and make it clear why I am more than capable of giving your grandmother effective advice.

You know I work for a top-five firm, and I'm sure you know my career progress. I'm hopefully on track to one day make partnership.'

She could hear the fervour in her voice and so it seemed could he.

'And that's the holy grail?'

'Yes,' she said simply. 'But the important thing is that I know my way around corporate law.

'However I'm assuming any one of the people you are meeting today is equally qualified on paper. I'm *guessing* you are trying to work out which of us would suit your grandmother most, at this time when she is recovering and more vulnerable than she usually is. So, yes, I know I can give your grandmother expert legal advice, but only you can decide *if* I am the right person to do it. I don't want the job unless I am.'

There was a silence and she saw surprise deepen in his brown eyes as a faint frown developed, one she needed to dispel. She didn't want him to think she didn't want the job.

'Look, I do want you to choose me. Of course I do. But I completely understand that, as it should be, your priority is for your grandmother to have the right person with the right approach. Someone you can trust. And if I'm not that person it's better to know now. For Belle. And for you and for me.'

He nodded. 'Fair enough. I appreciate your take on it.'

'Then please ask anything you want.'

'Okay. What would you do if you had a differing opinion to Belle? Or disagreed with a strategy? Would you give her an honest opinion, including reservations?'

'I don't lie,' Chloe said.

'Ever?' he asked.

'Ever,' she replied. 'Lies can cause too much damage.' They could cause hurt, pain and tragedy. If she hadn't lied, her father and brother would be alive today.

Logan was looking at her differently now. To her surprise she saw an understanding in his eyes, or perhaps it was compassion, and she realised she was showing too much emotion. To diffuse the seriousness, she smiled.

'I know it sounds unlikely, a lawyer who doesn't lie, but I think trust is important. Without it too much can go wrong. So, to answer your question, yes, I would give your grandmother my opinion, but I would choose my words carefully, taking into consideration her state of health, both physical and emotional. I would do my best always to be truthful and not patronising. I'm not a "yes" woman and I am pretty sure your grandmother would show me the door in less than five minutes if she thought I was.'

'True enough.' The words were accompanied by another smile, and she had to focus not to react, though she was fairly sure her toes were curling. But it was hard not to smile back when she saw the way his face creased, and saw the warmth in his brown eyes. 'But I don't think she'll show you the door.' He drummed his fingers on the table, and then said, 'You've got the job.'

Chloe tried to keep the smile cool, professional, as though it was no more than her due, but she couldn't quite manage it; her smile widened to a grin. But, damn it, she was pleased. This was a real chance to get ahead.

Innate honesty forced her to acknowledge that the sense of pride, of satisfaction, was mixed with something else—a sense of anticipation that had something to do with Logan. *Ridiculous.* Logan was simply a go-between—there would be little need to see much of him from now on in. Belle Jamieson was the client.

'Thank you,' she said. 'I truly appreciate the opportunity and I will do my best.'

'I'll hold you to it.' He rose to his feet. 'I'll be in touch to arrange a meeting, sooner rather than later.'

As Chloe walked round her desk to show him out, awareness jolted through her and, without meaning to, she found her gaze lingering on the swell of muscle under the lightweight jacket and the easy, lithe strength he exuded.

'Then I'll look forward to hearing from you. Thank you, Logan.'

As he reached the door, he turned and, with barely perceptible hesitation, held out his hand. Chloe looked down at it, absorbing the strength of his fingers, the shape of his forearm, and every instinct told her not to touch, even as she knew there was no choice.

She forced herself to clasp his hand and... *kaboom!* The touch kickstarted the simmering sense of desire into life, and she sensed the shockwave travel through her. She wrenched her gaze away only to see her own shock mirrored in his brown eyes and felt heat blush her cheeks. And still her hand was in his, she wasn't pulling it away and he wasn't dropping it.

Her lips parted slightly and then she blinked sharply.

Let go of his damned hand, Chloe.

But, even then, they stood just looking at each other, until finally she let go and he stepped backwards.

'Um…well. It's been great. Talk later?'

Pulling herself together, she nodded. 'Sure. Looking forward to it.' And, God help her, she meant it.

CHAPTER TWO

LOGAN FORCED HIS feet to move, made his way to the door and told himself that he was over-reacting. But he knew from the tingling in his fingers, the knot of desire in his gut, that he wasn't. Knew that this attraction was real and it was a live wire.

Doubt hit him—had he let that attraction bias him, let it affect his decision making?

It was a doubt he forced himself to consider as he strode towards the Tube station and one that he dismissed. Yes, like it or not, there had been a buzz of mutual awareness incited by a mere touch of her hand, one that still lingered now. But it was not an attraction he had any intention of acting on and he was pretty sure it hadn't impacted his decision.

His motivation had been to find the best so-licitor for Belle, because Logan would move heaven and earth to make sure his grandmother was happy and untroubled. Because it could make the difference between life and death. The doctors had been clear—Belle needed to be kept calm and happy, and needed to recuperate to give her the best chance of surviving the operation. Logan had every intention of making that happen.

And he had found the right person. Chloe Edwards had got it. She understood his criteria went beyond technical brilliance and paper qualifications. Chloe was smart, principled and undoubtedly qualified for the job. The right decision had been made and, as for the attraction, it was neither here nor there. Apart from introducing Chloe to his grandmother, he wouldn't need to see her again. The idea strangely unappealing.

He arrived at the door of Belle's London townhouse a short time later, where she was currently surrounded by a team of twenty-four-hour nursing care. In addition to this, Logan had moved in; the nurses were wonderful and necessary but he wanted to be at hand in case his grandmother needed him. His father should be here too, damn it. Somehow he had to locate Matt.

He walked softly towards Belle's room,

hesitated when he heard the murmur of voices and stopped when he heard the sound of his name. He looked through the ajar door and saw his grandmother sitting up in the bed, a nurse in her mid-fifties beside her.

'Ach, don't be distressed, Ms Jamieson.'

'I'll be distressed if I want, Hilda.' Bella's voice held an uncharacteristic note of petulance. 'And you shouldn't complain.'

The nurse shook her head. 'I wasn't complaining. I was just answering your questions. You asked about my family.'

'Yes, and you said you were worried. Worried because your son has fallen in love, worried because he is having a baby. How can that worry you?' Belle's voice was high with emotion, a strength of feeling that caused Logan to frown. It was important for Belle to be calm.

'It's only because they are so young. But perhaps you're right, Ms Jamieson; perhaps I am making too much of it.'

The nurse's voice was soothing, but to no avail. 'Don't patronise me. *Listen* to me.' Belle's hand reached out and covered the nurse's arm. 'You are going to be a grandmother; your child has found love, *wants* a family… Be glad of it. I would do anything if my grandson could find the same. My son nearly did, but…' Bella's voice cracked. 'I wish, I truly wish, I could have seen Logan happy before I die.'

'There'll be no talk of dying.'

'I'm not a fool. I know the risks of this operation and I know too that I'd go into it happier if I knew he was settled. Happy. That there was a chance the line would continue. But mostly I don't want to leave him alone.'

There was real agitation in his grandmother's voice now and Logan finally unfroze. He made to push open the door and then stopped, knowing instinctively that Belle would not want him to have heard that, to have seen her vulnerable. And so he soundlessly moved away, his head whirling, every protective instinct in him on alert.

There had been no doubting the sincerity in her voice or the genuine angst and Logan understood it. How could he not, given the complexities of their family history, given that his mother had died giving birth to Logan so that 'the line could continue'? It was a fact he'd discovered when he'd been six years old.

It was one of the rare times when his father

had actually been there, so the usual bedtime rules had been relaxed. He'd fallen asleep on the sofa, his presence forgotten, awoken to the sound of raised voices and blinked away sleep.

'You're his dad—you need to be here more for him!'

Logan had heard the fervency in Belle's tone and he'd really started to listen. 'I can't. Every time I see him, I think of Lisa, of what I lost. Hell, what she lost. So don't lecture me. Just remember that it was all your fault. He was your idea, remember?'

His dad's voice had been taut, edgy, and full of an indefinable weariness.

'That is not what happened, Matt.' Belle's voice had dropped then, gentled. 'Yes, I encouraged Lisa to have a baby, but only because she brought up the idea.'

'So you say.' Matt's voice had been flat. 'But until she talked to you, until you spoke about being a family, about continuing the line, Lisa and I didn't want a child. We were happy with each other. Then you interfered, because you wanted your legacy to continue.'

'I didn't interfere. I gave my opinion. Was it so wrong to hope we could become a real

THEIR MAURITIUS WEDDING RUSE

family, so wrong to want a grandchild, to want the line to continue?'

'"The line"? *Your* line is what you wanted, and so you hoped for a child who would be like you. Because I am not like you—I have always been a disappointment.'

'That's not fair or true.' Belle's voice had broken. 'I have always loved you and I couldn't have known what would happen to Lisa.'

'Doesn't matter. My wife, my Lisa, she died, Mum—died so you could have a grandchild. Because you persuaded her, blackmailed her emotionally—for all I know even monetarily.'

'That's not...that's not what happened.' Belle's voice had faltered. 'Lisa's death was nobody's blame or fault. Not mine, not yours and definitely not Logan's.'

But to Logan, listening hidden beneath a blanket, even though the nuances and words would only make proper sense over time, one thing had been plain: his birth had killed his mother and that meant it *was* his fault. If it hadn't been for him, his mother would be alive and his father would be happy. But now his father wasn't happy. He didn't make his father happy...and likely never could. The pain had seared deep into his psyche, into his very soul.

After that, Logan had stopped asking his father to stay, stopped begging Matt to take him with him on his travels. He had accepted the bitter truth: his presence caused his father pain. His father blamed Belle for his wife's death. Whether rightly or wrongly was sometimes a toss-up, he'd thought as he'd grown older.

But one thing Logan did know, then and now, was that Belle had been there for him and his father hadn't. Belle loved him; she didn't blame him for his mother's passing, and she had always done her best for him, bringing him up with love and security. She'd done her best to make up for his father's absence in his life. For that he owed her his love, even if he hadn't been able to give her the security of agreeing to be heir to the business, to be her successor at the helm.

He couldn't do that. He knew to do so would be to betray his mother's memory, and make truth out of his father's claim that she had died so Belle could have a worthy heir. He also knew, deep down, that it would make it impossible ever to have a relationship with his father and would ensure he never saw Matt again, rather than for the occasional visits he did now.

But there must be something he could do for Belle. Now, when she was facing death, she was worried about Logan and his future, and wanted to see him settled. The idea was impossible because he didn't want love and commitment, not when he had seen the risks they carried with them, seen what happened when love was taken away. His father's life had been blighted, the loss of his wife rendering him unable to love his own son or forgive his mother.

And Logan and Belle had suffered. Logan never wanted to hurt other people in that way. He figured he'd caused enough hurt already. It was safer for him to be on his own. It wouldn't be fair for him to achieve love, a happy relationship or a family when his birth had taken that opportunity from his parents.

But he knew he wouldn't be able to get Belle to see that because she still believed in love as a force for good. Her distress echoed in his head, along with what the doctors had said. He had to do something.

He moved along the corridor and slipped into his bedroom, sat on the bed and swung up his legs, his mind racing. Maybe seeing her son would set Belle's mind at rest. Pulling out his phone, he checked again to see if his dad had messaged. *Nada.* All his own messages still sat unacknowledged. What else could he do?

Logan drummed his fingers on the bed, and an idea sprang into his brain, an idea so out there that he dismissed it out of hand. But it wouldn't go away. Instead it fizzed, crackled and popped as his brain started assessing the idea, weighing up the pros, the cons, the risks, and the costs, considering and discarding options until finally, an hour later, Logan Jamieson had a plan.

Chloe looked up from her laptop as her phone rang. She glanced at the screen and her heart gave a sudden hop, skip and jump as she saw the caller's name: Logan.

Get over yourself.

'Hello, Chloe Edwards speaking.'

'Chloe. It's Logan. Apologies for calling so late but I need to talk to you.'

His voice was deep, sending a sudden frisson over her skin as it brought back memories of the scorch of his fingers around hers.

'Sure. When were you thinking of? I've got my work diary here...'

'Actually, I meant now. If you're free.'

'Now?'

'Yes. If you haven't eaten, we could go out for dinner?'

'Dinner?' She really did have to get a grip before he decided he'd made a terrible mistake and hired a parrot rather than a brilliant, top-notch lawyer. 'Could you give me some sort of idea what this is about? Is Belle alright?'

'I need some legal advice. Confidential legal advice.'

'Is this for your company, rather than Belle's?'

'It's more...personal.'

The word thrilled through her, even as she told herself not to be daft. If Logan wanted to ask her on a date, he would hardly pretend he needed legal advice. And, even if he was asking her out, her answer would be a categoric no. Logan was a client—or, at least, the grandson of a client. More than that, Chloe didn't date. Anyone. A decision made after her one disastrous attempt at a relationship, the memories of which still sent waves of bitter regret through her. Never again. That was a decision set in stone.

As for here and now, there was only one way to figure out what the hell was going on. 'OK. I know a good Italian restaurant. Why don't you join me there?' she suggested. That way it would be her local territory.

'That sounds like a plan.'

A plan that Chloe felt less than one hundred percent sure about an hour later as she saw Logan push open the door of the restaurant and enter. Perhaps she should have chosen a different place, somewhere more professional than the small, cosy, family-run Italian that she came to at least once a week. Maybe a different setting would have prevented the tummy flip as he headed towards her; any hope that she'd imagined his effect on her was quashed.

The man was still drop-dead gorgeous— blond hair still shower-damp, he was dressed now in a shirt over a pair of jeans with the sleeves rolled up exposing tanned, muscular forearms, jacket slung over one shoulder.

She rose to her feet, saw the way his gaze

THEIR MAURITIUS WEDDING RUSE

scanned her and saw a similar shellshocked expression in his brown eyes. She kept her hands resolutely by her side. No way would she risk a repeat of earlier.

'Hi.'

'Hi. Good choice of restaurant. It smells amazing in here.'

He sat and she followed suit. 'The food's pretty amazing too.'

The waiter approached the table and she grinned at him. 'Hi Carlos. How's it going?'

'Pretty good. And thanks for those study tips. I aced the test.' He handed Logan a menu as he spoke, but Logan shook his head.

'I'll have the same as Chloe,' he said and she sensed his contained energy, knowing that whatever he wanted to talk about was important.

'Two lasagnes and some sparkling water,' she requested, and Carlos smiled and nodded assent before walking away.

She turned to Logan then.

'Good choice,' he said.

'You could literally pick anything off this menu and you're guaranteed it's good. It always has been. I used to work here when I was younger.'

She'd stumbled across it one day aged sixteen, when her life had still been a daily hell of grief, remorse and pain. A time when she hadn't been eating properly, functioning properly and had had no plan. She'd walked past, and perhaps the appetising smells had drawn her in, because she'd entered. The owners, Lucio and his wife Maria, had sat her down and given her a pizza on the house. It had been a life changer. She'd ended up working for them and it had given her purpose, an escape from her home, which her mother was turning into a shrine to her father and brother.

'But we're not here to talk about food.'

'No, we're not. But, to be clear I am asking your legal advice, not your firm's—this whole conversation is in a private, personal capacity.'

Chloe frowned. 'I'm not allowed to take on any clients on a personal basis.'

'This is me, as a private individual.'

'I understand but my partners wouldn't.' She raised a hand before he could speak. 'But I'll happily give you my advice in a private capacity for free.'

He nodded and then sat back as Carlos returned with their food and drinks. As they thanked the waiter, poured the water and tasted the first mouthful, she sensed that he was taking one final moment to make sure he really wanted to go ahead, and her curiosity intensified.

'I need to give you some background before I cut to the chase. You already know that my grandmother had a heart attack.'

She nodded.

'Now she has two options ahead of her. She can do nothing, take medication and hope for the best, or she can have an operation. At her age the operation is high risk, but if she makes it through her quality of life will be much better. She has opted for the operation route.'

'That must be scary,' Chloe said.

'She says she isn't scared of dying, she's scared of fading away, getting weaker and weaker.'

'I meant it must be scary for you,' she said softly. 'You are obviously very close.'

She could see it in his eyes, in the tension in his jaw and shoulders, and she had a sudden urge to reach out, smooth away the worry, stand and knead away the knots in his shoulders. 'It's not easy to think about losing someone you love.'

'No,' he said softly. 'And that means I want to do everything I can to ensure I don't lose her.' Determination made of steel etched his voice and features.

'And you have figured out a way to do it that requires legal advice?' Chloe frowned. 'I'm sorry Logan but I think there will be a conflict of interest here. I shouldn't really be discussing Belle like this. She's my client.'

'I understand, but please just hear me out. I promise this is all in Belle's best interests.'

There was no doubting that and after a moment Chloe nodded. 'I'll listen but I am not promising anything.'

'Thank you. To summarise, Belle's medical team have advised me that one of the most important things for her is to make sure she is calm and happy and in the best frame of mind before the operation. Equally, if there is any chance she isn't going to survive the operation, I want to know that her last week was full of happiness.'

'I get that. I promise I will do all I can to put her mind at rest about her legal affairs. But this isn't about that, is it?'

'No. This is about me. Belle wants to feel that I am settled and happy. She wants there to be hope for the future, a chance that her bloodline will continue.'

Chloe blinked, trying to sort out her thoughts. 'Are you in a relationship? Do you want me to draft some sort of pre-nup?'

'Nope. I'm not in a relationship.'

'So what do you need me for?'

'I'm going to fake it,' Logan said.

'Fake wh—?' Chloe broke off. 'Fake a relationship?' she asked.

'Yes.'

'But that's nuts… I mean, it won't work.'

'Why not?'

'Because I'm sure your grandmother is nobody's fool. She'll suspect if you conveniently turn up with a girlfriend.'

'She won't. She doesn't know that I know this is what she wants—I overheard a conversation. She doesn't even know I was in the house at the time. My plan is to introduce my "fiancée" and tell her that I wasn't sure if she'd approve, because she hasn't actually approved of any of my relationships so far, but in the end I decided I wanted her to meet the woman I intend to settle down with.

My grandmother is a romantic—she may be ruthless in the boardroom, but she truly believes in love. That's why she got married three times. The "whirlwind romance" idea will work. Plus, it doesn't have to work for long. Belle's operation is in ten days. All I have to do is introduce my fiancée and then maybe have one more meeting after that.'

There was no ounce of doubt in his voice.

'I get it. I really do. You want her to be happy. But I wouldn't advise it. I assume you're going to pay someone and you want a contract drafted. I can recommend someone to do that, but it's dynamite. The person you pay, she'll…well…she'll have you over the proverbial barrel. All she has to do is threaten to show Belle the contract, and then what?'

'I thought of that. It would have to be someone I trust.'

'Do you have a someone in mind?'

'Yes,' he said simply. 'I want you to do it. I want you to be my fake fiancée.'

CHAPTER THREE

CHLOE BLINKED, THEN BLINKED again as her brain scrambled to absorb the words.

'Me?' She could hear incredulity in her tone. 'That's ridiculous. Even more ridiculous than the idea itself. There is no way I can do that.'

'Why not?' His voice was the epitome of reason. 'Unless…' For the first time, doubt registered in his eyes. 'Unless you're in a relationship. I should have asked that first.'

'I'm not in a relationship. I haven't been for a while.'

And wouldn't be again. Couldn't be again. Almost against her will, her mind revisited the debacle with Mike. It had all started so well… Mike had ticked all the boxes and they'd shared similar goals—his holy grail being a partnership in a top accountancy firm—but best of all her mother had liked

Mike. She had approved, encouraged the relationship and for the first time since the tragedy Chloe had felt a bit closer to her, a faint echo of how it had once been back when she had felt cared for.

So, she'd invested everything in Mike, sure that 'love' would happen in its own time. But it hadn't, not for her anyway, and she had been sure not for Mike either. Then one day out of the blue Mike had suggested moving in together because it 'made sense financially' and 'would be a good test of compatibility'—then maybe they could consider 'putting things on a more permanent footing'.

Then he'd told her he loved her. Shock had rendered her speechless but in that moment of impact she'd realised what should have been obvious before: love was never going to happen for her, because Chloe didn't believe in it, not for her. Because she had destroyed love on so many levels; she had been an instrument in bringing pain, loss and death.

How could she possibly offer or receive love? The answer had been that she couldn't. And in trying to do so she'd caused more pain. She had tried to explain to Mike that it was a deficiency in her, not him, but he hadn't understood. He had been humiliated and angry, and Chloe had felt further guilt burn that she'd caused someone pain. Again.

But there had been worse to come. Her mother's reaction to the news had been something else Chloe hadn't seen coming—she hadn't read the signs.

Janet Edwards had looked at her, her expression stricken, as she'd said, 'Why did you reject him? You could have got married...you could have had a child. A son. You could have called him James, after your brother. Maybe he'd even look like him.'

And far too late the penny had dropped with a clang as to why Janet had liked Mike so much, why she'd approved. When she'd seen fresh disappointment on her mother's face, she had seen she'd failed her yet again. She'd known that she could never risk a relationship again and wouldn't risk hurting another man, or raising her mother's hopes.

So now she could look Logan straight in the eye and say categorically, 'That isn't the reason I can't do it. I can't do it because it is a terrible idea.'

'I understand you're surprised,' he said. His voice was unoffended, calm and full of confidence that didn't seem at all dented by her words. 'When I first thought of it, I thought I was possibly—'

'A few sandwiches short of a picnic?' she offered.

'Well, a bit out there. But the more I thought about it, the more I realised that what I had was equivalent to a luxury picnic hamper.'

'How exactly did you work that out?' Chloe realised she did really want to know.

'You said that I needed someone I can trust. I can trust you.'

'You don't know that. You don't know me.'

'I know I trusted you with my grandmother.'

'As a lawyer...which is my job. It doesn't mean you can trust me with this. I'd advise you not to trust anyone with this.'

'Not acceptable. I am going to do this—I have to. You're right, I don't know you, but it makes sense to trust you. Or at least to risk it.'

'Why?'

'Instinct backed by logic. You told me becoming a partner is your holy grail.'

'Yes, it is.'

'Then you are very unlikely to threaten to tell Belle the truth or try and blackmail me.

You wouldn't want to lose a client of Belle's prestige. *That's* why I can trust you.'

'It's also why I can't do it. Belle is my client.'

'And you're worried that, once she's on the road to recovery and I tell her the truth, she'll fire you.' He shook his head. 'She won't. I'll make that good. Belle will understand that this was my idea, that I persuaded you to do it.'

Chloe shook her head. 'That's not the point. Belle would be right to sack me. Belle is my client and I would be lying to her. That is unethical. And, as I told you earlier, I don't lie. Because lies do have consequences.' She knew that with bone-deep knowledge. 'I can't be part of this.'

'I do understand that lies have consequences. It's not something I take lightly. One of Belle's favourite proverbs is "what a tangled web we weave when we practise to deceive". She told me that there was never a need to lie to her, and in return she wouldn't lie to me. And as far as I know she has kept that deal.'

Though Chloe was sure she heard a soupçon of doubt in his voice and wondered if

Logan was as sure as he wanted to be. Not her business.

'Then why start now?'

'Because now there *is* a need to lie to her. Not for myself, but for Belle. This lie is not designed to hurt, or for gain, or to cheat. This lie is woven from love and a desire to do good. At worst it could make the last weeks of my grandmother's life happy ones. But hopefully at best it could send her into her operation in the best frame of mind, optimistic and happy, and that could help her get through it.'

The words were said calmly but with an intensity, a certainty, that triggered a whole new response in Chloe, a realisation of how important this was. And with that came a sudden sharp flare of anxiety. What if she refused and she caused another death? What if this would be the crucial factor and her part in it, the decision she made here, might mean Belle didn't make it through? Would it be her fault…?

She forced herself to unclench her hands, aware that her whole body was taut and that panic was a hair's breadth away.

Logan looked at her, a slight frown on his

48 THEIR MAURITIUS WEDDING RUSE

forehead, and then he shook his head, reached out a hand and gently covered hers.

'Jeez. I'm sorry, Chloe. This is not your call or your responsibility. I am doing this whether you agree or not. If it doesn't sit right with you, I will find someone else. I'm not trying to guilt you into this. I understand what a lot I am asking of you, that this entails a conflict that is a professional risk and also goes against what you are comfortable with on a personal level. I just truly believe that this is the best way to maximise Belle's chances. So it feels that this lie is okay, the exception to the rule.'

She looked down at his hand, oh, so aware of his touch and the warmth and irrational sense of comfort it gave her. She heard, too, the sincerity of the apology and the truth of his words. Now, as the panic receded, she was aware of the warmth burgeoning into something else; aware that she wanted him to leave his hand there, and that she wanted more.

'I'm not sure it works like that.'

'Belle is my grandmother, but she's more than that. She has been my rock—she's always been there for me my whole life. The least I can do for her now is this. Give her peace of mind when she needs it most. If that means I have to lie, then so be it. But I completely understand if you don't want to do it.'

Chloe stared at him, heard love in his voice and envied him. Because that family love was gone from her life. Before everything had gone so tragically wrong, her childhood had been happy, even if she'd sometimes felt excluded by her mother. Although she hadn't known when growing up, she'd been unplanned. Her mother would have been happy with one child, their 'golden boy', as her mother had always referred to James. But, despite James being the favourite, her mother had done her best and had shown Chloe affection.

And Chloe had adored her father. He had always been there for her, as if he'd been trying to make up for the fact that her brother was the favourite. He at least had tried to balance the family dynamic and had made an effort. He'd taken her for walks. When she was little, she'd splashed in puddles and when she was older she'd listened to him talk about his poetry, how he enjoyed writing even though his job gave him too little time.

As for James, as far as Chloe was concerned, he *had* been golden. A perfect older brother, he'd played with her, helped her with her homework, teased her and she'd loved him, with his sunny nature. He'd also been an A-grade student with minimal effort, had excelled at sport and made his way through university with ease. And, alongside all that, he'd been ambitious, driven, his aim to make money and be a success, a partner in the best law firm in London. In contrast, Chloe had been gawky, awkward, difficult...generally less loveable.

She could still remember her mother's anguished words at the funeral. 'Oh, God, why did it have to be James?' The inference had been clear and her teenaged self had stood there in the chasm of awkwardness, pain and despair as she'd realised that she'd lost everything, that there was no love left in the world for her.

So now, looking at Logan, she did envy him, and she also understood why he would do anything for the woman who had always been his 'rock'. She realised that she was actually considering the idea, and told herself to get a grasp of reality. How could she agree to something that was a lie, a lie that could cost her so much professionally, a lie that entailed deceiving a client,

'I'm flattered you trust me, but there must be someone else you trust more.'

'Maybe,' he said. 'But it's not only about trust. There's another reason I'm asking you.' For the first time since he'd sat down at the table, Logan looked a little awkward, a little unsure. Not a whole lot, but she was sure there was tension in his shoulders, a hint of doubt in his eyes as he sipped his water. 'Can I ask you a question?'

'Sure.'

Another pause, and then he asked, 'Am I imagining the attraction between us?'

Damn it. The unforeseen question weaved and danced across the table, the word 'attraction' simmering and shimmering in the air. Embarrassment threatened, along with an annoyance that she hadn't hidden her reaction to him better, and then the whole question with all its nuance hit her: Logan had said 'between us', which implied that this was a mutual attraction.

'Us?' she asked, her voice suddenly low and husky. 'Just to be clear, you're saying this is mutual? Assuming it exists at all,' she added hurriedly.

'It definitely exists on my side.'

She stared at him, then dipped her head. She couldn't help it as a flare, a thrill of sleek satisfaction, purred through her at the certainty in his voice.

'It exists on mine too,' she said softly, and now he smiled, but this smile was different—this had a hint of the predator in it—and there was pride, satisfaction, that matched her own as his brown eyes darkened. 'But I wish it didn't. Our relationship needs to be strictly professional.'

'Of course. I understand that.' Yet she was sure she heard the hint of regret in the undertone of the words. 'But it's very existence will make it easier for us to play a convincing couple for the short period of time we'd need to do it.'

Chloe couldn't help herself; for a moment she pictured them pretending to be a couple. Would they hold hands, would they stand close, would they kiss? Just the idea made her giddy, twisting her tummy, heating her skin. And how would they balance the now acknowledged reality of this attraction with the fact they weren't a couple? The whole idea was too complicated, however reasonable he made it sound. Whilst she got that Logan wasn't proposing a real relationship, even the pretence felt too risky, too tricky. There must be a different way.

'All you need to do is find another woman you can trust who you find attractive.'

He raised his eyebrows. 'Just like that? I don't know about you, but trust doesn't come that easy to me. Not when I am entrusting something as important as Belle's health and well-being to someone.'

The sheer simplicity of his words gave her pause as she recognised his point. Trust was imperative here. But how could she do it? How could she offer Belle professional advice whilst lying to her? Or was that an excuse? After all, Chloe knew the lie wouldn't impact the advice she gave, wouldn't bias her or affect it. Yet it would still be a lie. Years ago she had told lies and her father and brother had died in consequence.

But this lie was a lie born of love, an altruistic lie, the only motivation being to help, to make a life better, to even perhaps make a difference between life and death. Would help prolong Belle's life and make a differ-

54 THEIR MAURITIUS WEDDING RUSE

ence to her right here and now? Perhaps to take part in this lie would balance the scales, make some reparation for her past. And if she could help save a life that was more important than anything else, including her professional ethics and even her career.

'I'll do it,' she said. 'If you still want me.' Even as she said the words, she knew they'd come out wrong. She looked down, realised his hand was still covering hers and awareness surged.

'I still want you,' he said, and now goosebumps rippled her skin along with a shiver of desire.

Then she realised her previous questions were valid and she hadn't answered them. How was she going to handle this mutual attraction? She might as well ask herself the best way to play with fire. The answer was to not play at all and it was too late for that.

Yet, even as doubts burgeoned, so did anticipation. 'What now?' she asked.

Logan looked across the table at Chloe, relief that she had agreed, a knowledge of how much he was asking of her mixed with a sheer masculine satisfaction that the attraction went both ways. He blinked the emotions away.

Chloe was right: they needed to plan and so far he had to admit his plan was a little skimpy on detail.

'I'll take you to meet Belle. Introduce you as both a corporate lawyer and my fiancée. We'll keep it brief, and try to focus on the professional aspect.'

Chloe stared at him, opened her mouth and closed it again. 'You don't think that's a little sketchy? I mean, Belle may ask some questions. For example, how did we meet, when did we meet?'

'We'll say we met through work. I came in to see you on my own behalf a couple of months ago...cue whirlwind romance. We got engaged just before her heart attack, I didn't want to rock the boat by telling her, but now I want her to know.'

He could see Chloe didn't look convinced.

'I doubt she'll want details, and if she does the beauty of a whirlwind courtship is that we don't need to know much about each other. We can wing it.'

'Said no corporate lawyer ever.' There was a small smile on her face but Logan could see the doubt that still shadowed her eyes. Understood it; after all, given the enormity of what she was doing she wanted to minimise the risks.

'Fair enough. How do you think we should prep?'

'We know nothing at all about each other. Knowing something would make it less awkward, more convincing.'

'Okay. When's your birthday?'

'Sixth of August. I'm twenty-six years old.'

'Where do you live?'

'Near here. In a one-bedroom flat.'

'Car?'

'No.'

Logan paused. There had been something in her voice, a fleeting expression in her hazel eyes he couldn't place.

Before he could say anything, she said quickly, 'What about your answers to the same questions?'

'Fifteenth of December, currently living with my grandmother, otherwise I also have an apartment in London, as well as Edinburgh and Sydney. I have three cars.' He smiled. 'There—we'll be fine. Truly. It's one brief meeting.'

'Yes, but even briefly we'll need to look like a convincing couple.'

'That's where we'll let the attraction come into play.'

Chloe shook her head. 'What does that mean, *exactly*? And why is it even a good idea? Even if this was real, I would want to present my professional side whilst emphasising that we love each other and that we're in it for the long term. I wouldn't be all over you.'

There was a small silence, one he hurried to breach. 'You're saying smouldering looks won't really cut it.'

'Exactly. Though...' A sudden impish smile tipped her lips. 'Out of interest, what does a "smouldering look" look like?'

He smiled back, arrested by the teasing glint in her hazel eyes, and now his gaze was caught and he looked at her—really looked at her.

Her hair was loose, a glossy strawberry-blonde cascade that caught the rays of the late setting sun through the window, highlighting motes of red and gold. Hazel eyes fringed with dark lashes met his, and a slight blush tinged her cheekbones. His gaze dropped to her lips, lips that looked so goddamned kissable... And now he didn't even try to look smouldering, he simply let show on his face how he felt, in his eyes, and he saw her hazel eyes darken and linger on his lips as her own lips parted.

Before she gave a slightly shaky laugh. 'Right, um, probably best we avoid any smoulder.'

He nodded, still slightly poleaxed, still desperate to lean across the table and complete what had been set into motion. But he wouldn't. This was complicated enough; letting attraction rule would complicate it further. The most important person was Belle and he mustn't, wouldn't, forget that. He wouldn't blur the lines or muddy the water. This had to stay professional.

'Yes. Right.' He cleared his throat. 'No smoulder.' *Professional does it.* 'And if you draw up a contract I'm good with that. Also, you need to name your fee.'

'No.' The word came out instantly. 'I don't want a fee. It…wouldn't feel right.'

'Then let me donate something to a charity of your choice.'

Chloe considered that for a minute, clearly running it through her ethical odometer, and then she said, 'That could work. But first let's see how it all goes. Any form of payment doesn't sit right with me.'

'Fine. But you will need a ring.'

'I can't let you buy me a ring.'

'Said no real fiancée ever…' he pointed out.

'I meant, I can use one of my own.'

He shook his head. 'That wouldn't sit right with *me*. It needs to be the sort of ring I would buy for you, one that my grandmother will look at and know it feels authentic. I'll sort it out before we meet my grandmother tomorrow.'

'Tomorrow?'

'Yes.' Further doubts clouded her eyes and he kept his voice confident. 'We'll be good.' They had to be. He would not let his grandmother down. He would do anything to increase the chances of the operation working. 'We'll meet in the morning, then head to Belle's.'

CHAPTER FOUR

ANTICIPATION, NERVES AND a sense of surrealness mingled the following morning as Chloe waited for Logan to arrive to pick her up. Wished she'd managed to come up with an excuse not to have to get into a car with him, or rather not to get into a car at all. The morning ahead fraught enough without the added anxiety of a car journey. She had never even learnt how to drive, too governed by the fear of causing another accident, and avoided cars wherever she could.

Looking down at the quiet residential London street, she saw a sleek, low-slung sports car pull up outside and she headed for the door, taking one quick double take of her reflection in the hallway mirror. She'd chosen to dress professionally for the meeting in a cream blouse tucked into dark-blue trousers topped with a jacket. As a concession to the dual role she was playing, she'd left her hair loose.

Not for the first time, she wondered why she'd agreed to this idea, and yet she felt no regret and knew she would make the same decision again. As she left her building, glancing up at the early morning sky, seeing the joggers, headphones on as they ran, she hoped her decision hadn't been swayed by the attraction, the sparking, jolting, sensations Logan evoked, the sense of being alive, of yearning, of need.

She saw him now, standing by the gleaming silver vehicle, and her breath hitched in her throat. The man was...a glorious specimen of humanity; there was no two ways about it. She drank in the unruly, thick blond hair, the jut of his nose, the deep-brown eyes, the sculpted features and even more sculpted muscles. And exactly as she had frozen to the spot, so it seemed had he, his dark eyes intent, focused. She forced herself to break the spell and stepped forward.

'Good morning.'

'Good morning.'

She took a deep breath and climbed into the

car, focusing on keeping her breathing even as he followed suit.

'You ready?'

'As ready as I'll ever be.'

'Good. But first...' He reached into the glove compartment and pulled out a jewellery box. Despite the knowledge that this was nothing more than a prop, a sense of anticipation rippled through Chloe, along with a sudden sliver of regret that this would never happen to her for real. Which didn't even make sense, because she didn't want love or commitment—that wasn't on her bucket list, her to-do list, or any list. She'd never want the responsibility of holding someone's happiness, never want to raise hopes in her mother she couldn't fulfil.

As her eyes scanned the box, she glanced up at Logan, wondering what he was thinking, but knew it wasn't the time to ask. Perhaps it never would be. After all, it didn't matter. This was business, a deal without vows.

In a deft movement, he flicked open the box and she gave a small gasp. The ring was stunning, not over the top but distinct and unique, a glitter and sparkle of brilliant green and ice-white. 'Peridot and diamond—peridot is your birth stone and I thought it matched the green in your eyes.'

An inexplicable tear threatened, even as she told herself again that it was just a prop. Then he took the ring out and laid it in the palm of her hand, and the brush of his fingers took her breath away.

'I hope you like it.'

'I love it,' she said. Carefully she took the ring out and slipped it onto the ring finger of her left hand. She held it up in the sunlight that streamed through the window. 'I know you did it to look the part for Belle but...'

'No.' His voice was low. 'I bought this for you because I hoped you'd like it. Because I truly do appreciate what you are doing here. I know you have reservations and you're doing it anyway, and that means a lot to me. I know this ring isn't a real engagement ring, or a lifetime commitment, but it is a token of my appreciation and in that it is genuine.'

His words touched her and brought another incipient tear to her eye, prompting a fierce blink. She did not cry; there was no reason to cry. 'Thank you,' she said. 'And I may have reservations, but I don't regret my choice. For what it's worth, I think what you are doing is a truly good thing, and I will do my best to play my part in it.'

And without even thinking she leaned forward and brushed her lips against his cheek, wanting to show her appreciation for his thoughtfulness. But as she inhaled the woodsy, citrus scent of him, felt the warmth of his body, something happened: the sense of appreciation morphed into awareness of his proximity, the *heat* of his body, the closeness of his lips. And as she moved backwards their gazes locked.

She saw his eyes darken, heard his breath catch and all she wanted to do was lean forward again, but this time she wanted a different kind of kiss as desire strummed a tune of temptation and yearn. But she didn't succumb and neither did he. Perhaps it was the sun going behind a cloud that brought common sense to the fore, but somehow she forced her eyes to break the gaze, forced her body to turn away.

She pulled on her seatbelt with a decisive click and told herself it was nothing more than an ill-timed moment, to put it behind her and pretend it hadn't happened. Because it was imperative to keep the professional line firmly drawn in the shifting sands of desire.

She took a deep breath. 'Have you told Belle anything?'

'Not yet. She was still asleep when I left the house, but the nurse said she had a good night.' He started the engine and Chloe pushed down the sense of panic, unable now even to pinpoint its cause, as nerves tautened and tightened. She looked down as he reached out and placed a hand over hers in a swift reassuring clasp. 'You're going to be fine. *We're* going to be fine.'

He was right. He had to be. This had to work. For Belle Jamieson's sake.

Half an hour later, Logan pushed open the front door to Belle's townhouse and they entered. He turned, opened the door to one of the reception rooms, showed Chloe inside and gave what he hoped was a reassuring smile. Though in truth he found it hard to put their near-kiss behind them, his whole body still on alert, his libido not yet stood down.

Focus, Logan.

He would not let himself be distracted from the purpose of this meeting. 'I'll go ahead and prepare the ground and then I'll be straight back to take you in.'

She nodded, and as he headed for the door she said, 'Logan?'

He turned and she moved towards him, reaching out and gently touching his arm in a fleeting gesture. 'It's going to be okay,' she said. 'We'll pull this off.'

A warmth touched him at her smile, the realisation that she was trying to reassure him as well. Her words were a mantra he repeated in his head as he walked down the corridor and entered Belle's room.

The nurse rose to her feet. 'I'll give you some time together,' she said and headed to the door.

'Thank you.' Logan smiled and walked to the bed. His grandmother looked better than when he'd last seen her through the crack in the door, but she still looked a long way from the Belle Jamieson he was used to. She was sitting up in the bed, propped up by cushions, and as he leaned down and kissed her cheek a surge of protective love washed over him and cemented the determination to pull it off.

'Have you found me a solicitor?' Belle asked.

'I have. I've brought her with me this morning but, before I bring her in, to meet you there is something I need to explain.'

He paused and Belle surveyed him with slightly narrowed eyes, eyes that were brighter now with curiosity, and seeing that interest motivated Logan to go on as Belle said, 'Just say it, Logan. I can take it.'

'Her name is Chloe Edwards. She's a corporate lawyer for a top-five firm and she definitely knows what she's talking about. A rising star...' He paused for impact and to give himself one last chance to change his mind.

'And?' Belle asked.

'And she is also my fiancée.' There was silence and he could almost hear the whir and cog of his grandmother's brain; he saw the dawn of suspicion in her expression. 'That's where I was yesterday,' he added. 'With Chloe, trying to work out whether we should tell you or not.'

His grandmother imperceptibly relaxed. Hopefully the idea that he hadn't been in the house would be enough to allay any suspicion that he'd overheard her conversation.

'Why wouldn't you tell me?'

68 THEIR MAURITIUS WEDDING RUSE

'I wasn't sure how you'd feel about the idea of me being engaged and, given how close your operation is, I wasn't sure if I should rock the boat.' Logan smiled now. 'You've hardly approved of any of my previous girlfriends, have you?'

Belle snorted. 'That's because you didn't care a snap of your fingers for any of them. And the last one was an airhead.'

'Chloe is definitely not an airhead,' Logan said. 'And I do care a snap of my fingers for her.' It occurred to Logan that that was true. 'And I definitely care about you. I don't want anything to upset you, but I do want you to meet Chloe, because she is the best corporate lawyer I know, but also because she is my fiancée.'

'Well, bring her in, then. I won't eat her.' Belle sat up straighter and Logan could see the bloom of healthy colour in her cheeks, her blue eyes sparkling, and satisfaction surged through him. Belle already looked better than she had in weeks.

Logan left the room, re-entered the reception room and found Chloe looking down at her phone. 'I'm doing a word game,' she said.

'As the alternative was to pace a hole in your grandmother's carpet. How is she?'

'Waiting to meet you. She's assured me she won't eat you.'

'Well, that's reassuring.' Chloe tugged down her jacket and took a deep breath. 'Right. Let's do this.'

They entered Belle's room next to each other, and Chloe went straight forward towards his grandmother whilst Logan stood back, sensing she would prefer that.

'Hello. I'm Chloe Edwards.'

'Lawyer and fiancée,' Belle said.

'Yes.' Chloe smiled. 'I am both those things, but I would understand if you didn't want to consult me professionally as the former, given that I am also the latter.' She took a deep breath. 'It is my duty to give you unbiased professional advice but if you prefer I can recommend a colleague.'

It was maybe in that moment Logan truly understood what he had asked of Chloe. True, he'd promised her his own business, but it would go against her grain to have to recommend one of her colleagues, a peer and most likely a rival, whose holy grail was probably also partnership.

Chloe continued without a beat. 'Now that's out of the way, I'd like to say that it is amazing to meet you. You were an inspiration to me, and I also love Belle's products. But, most important, I know how much you mean to Logan.'

There was a sincerity in Chloe's voice that couldn't be missed and he saw Belle relax slightly against the pillows as she turned to Logan. 'Logan, stop dawdling at the door and come in. Sit down, both of you.'

They complied. Without even thinking, Logan reached out to touch Chloe's hand and she glanced across at him with a quick smile.

'Tell me about yourself.' Belle's voice was stronger and her gaze intent as she looked at Chloe. Logan felt himself relax as he saw the way Chloe leant forward and started to talk. He saw Belle nod in approval as the conversation progressed, heard Belle laugh as Chloe described the first time she'd worn make-up and watched his grandmother study and admire the ring.

After a while, Belle smiled up at him, then looked across to Chloe. 'So the two of you are sure?'

'I'm sure,' Logan said, the words no more than the truth.

'And so am I,' Chloe chimed in.

'I'm glad.' His grandmother smiled at both of them and Logan felt a sense of jubilation. This was working.

Then Belle sat up straighter and her blue eyes positively gleamed as she tapped her fingers on the blanket in thought, looking from one to the other of them. 'You were right to tell me. Because it means I can do what I've always wanted.'

'What's that?' Logan felt a faint flicker of foreboding.

'I want to be at your wedding.' Belle's voice was resolute. 'And I'm not risking dying first. So we have a week to plan your wedding. It's going to be the most beautiful ceremony in the world.'

Logan felt shock freeze on his face as his mind scrambled to catch up with events. He hadn't seen this coming and clearly, from the quickly concealed horror on her face, neither had Chloe.

Belle beamed as she continued. 'We can have it in Mauritius.' She glanced up at Chloe. 'I don't know if you've been there or not?'

Chloe shook her head, clearly not trusting herself to speak.

'It's beautiful,' Belle said softly. 'I grew up there, I fell in love for the first time there, and I came up with the ideas for Belle's there. I took Logan there as a child. Truly, it's a perfect venue. I know it's your wedding, Chloe, but I hope you'll consider it.'

It was time to intervene. 'Hang on a minute,' Logan said. 'This is not a feasible plan.'

'Why not?' Logan recognised the steely tone in his grandmother's voice and part of him, the part that wasn't busy panicking, rejoiced in it. This sounded like pre-stroke Belle, the grandmother he'd been worried had gone for good. 'It sounds pretty feasible to me unless you don't want me at the wedding.'

'Of course I...of course we do. But you have an operation in ten days. You are meant to be resting and recuperating.'

'And I will be. You two lovebirds can go to Mauritius and get it all planned and sorted. I'll rest here. Then I'll fly out for the wedding.'

'You can't. It's a twelve-hour flight minimum.' Next to him he sensed Chloe give a small flinch, presumably contemplating how daft it was for Belle to contemplate such a thing.

'What's the point of having money if you don't spend it? I'll be accompanied by the best medical team money can buy and I'll take every precaution imaginable. This is my life—don't I get to choose how I spend what may be the last days of it? I want to see Mauritius again. It's a place that holds some of my best memories and to see you married there... It matters to me, Logan.'

'But...' Chloe started, and Logan looked at her, a warning in his eyes. Perhaps he should close this down, but he wasn't sure what that would do to his grandmother.

Belle turned to Chloe and held out a hand. 'I know that this may not be the wedding you'd planned, and I truly know it is a big ask,' she said. 'But later, in a few months, we can hold another event, a ceremony...the wedding of your dreams.'

'That wasn't what I was going to say,' Chloe said softly. 'Like Logan, I was thinking about the risk to you. And I was thinking about Logan—if anything were to go wrong, he would blame himself.'

'He would have nothing to blame himself

74 THEIR MAURITIUS WEDDING RUSE

for,' Belle said. 'It is my idea and my risk to take.'

She reached out and took Logan's hand in hers. 'My risk and my responsibility. If these are my last days on earth then I am entitled to live them as I choose. And this is what I choose. Your news has already rejuvenated me. I feel stronger, better... You've given me something to live for.

'But I do still want to retain Chloe's professional services, so perhaps we could meet before you fly out. Plus, I promise, if it is truly impossible for me to fly out, I'll attend by video link, but this is what I want—for you to get married in Mauritius before my operation.'

Logan looked down at the hand that covered his, heard the strength and determination in his grandmother's voice, saw the sparkle in her blue eyes and tried to decide what to do. Even as he recognised the enormity of what he wanted to do, he wanted to agree to the plan, however preposterous it was.

But this was a completely different proposition to what he and Chloe had agreed. This would be a marriage, a wedding, the necessity to prolong this façade, this illusion, for more than just a 'brief meeting'. This was pretence on a way bigger scale. How could he ask that of Chloe? But how could he not? He looked at Belle and saw the renewed vigour, and more than that the happiness on her face. How could he pull the rug?

This woman had done so much for him; she had been his bedrock, had brought him up with principles and provided security, love and laughter. She had never once blamed him for his unwitting part in the tragedy of his mother's death, or for being a constant reminder of the rift between Matt and her. She had never begrudged acting as surrogate parent. Belle was his family and he owed her so much. He'd already denied her one thing she wanted—he could not get involved with the company she was so proud of—but he could do this for her.

And that was why he heard his voice say the words, 'Then that's what we'll do.'

CHAPTER FIVE

HALF AN HOUR later they left the house.

'There's a park near here. Let's go there, and we can talk,' Logan suggested.

Once they were there and she was completely sure they were out of sight of Belle's house, Chloe stopped and turned to Logan.

'"Then that's what we'll do"?' she said, repeating his words, allowing every iota of incredulity to show in her tone, uncaring at the raised pitch. 'Why, why, why on earth did you agree?'

He led the way over to a bench. They sat and he turned to her, his expression serious. 'I know it's a massive ask, and I promise I understand the enormity of it, but—'

'There are no buts,' Chloe said flatly. 'It *is* a massive ask and the point here is that you didn't actually ask—you just agreed. You didn't even try to stop it. You could have pointed out the impracticalities—explained we don't want to rush into it, that we were planning a longer engagement, to make sure, said you have work commitments, suggested an engagement party... You must have been able to think of *something.*'

'I couldn't. Partly because she would have an answer for all those things. But mostly because... I could see the change in her.'

His voice was gruffer now, and Chloe could hear the emotion, even as she knew he was trying to smooth its edges.

'Since the heart attack she's been a shadow of her former self. I've never seen her so frail or vulnerable. Today, when she believed we are engaged—when she started to talk about Mauritius, about the wedding—she looked revitalised, more herself than she's been for weeks and... I couldn't pull the rug from under her feet. Not when I put the damn thing there.'

Her heart twisted at his words. She could hear the raw fear in his voice, the fear he was going to lose someone who clearly meant so much to him. He ran a hand through his hair. 'But I do see from your point of view there is no excuse.'

Chloe tried to summon further outrage but found that she couldn't. 'I do understand that your priority is Belle and her wellbeing. But...' Understanding didn't stem the sense of disbelief, of panic. 'I can't marry you,' she said flatly. It was a lie of too big proportion and would require them to weave a massive web of deceit. And it would entail spending more time with Logan and she wasn't sure how that would work.

'Will you hear me out before you make a final decision? Please.'

'Okay.' How could she refuse the request?

'If you agree I will keep the wedding completely private, no publicity. In a few weeks, we'll tell Belle the truth and get the marriage annulled. On a practical level, you can simply tell your work that Belle has taken you on and needs you to travel to Mauritius on work-related business. I'll tell Belle the only way we will agree to this wedding is if it is kept completely private because we want everything to be as calm as possible for the sake of her health.'

'But some people will have to know. Belle's medical team...and what about family?' Chloe knew nothing about Logan's family set-up; Belle Jamieson had always been tight-lipped about her private life. And Chloe's research had been centred on Belle's company.

'We will tell the medical team that she is going to Mauritius for sentimental reasons, to see the place where she grew up. As for family...' Logan's lips tightened. 'You don't need to worry about that. The only family involved here are Belle and myself.'

Chloe saw the set of his jaw, the reserve in his eyes and knew he wouldn't elaborate further. And she got that. She had no wish to discuss her family, her personal life, either. Yet she felt an urge to reach out, take his hand and offer comfort even though she didn't know what she'd be offering comfort for.

'Understood,' she said instead, rewarded by the tension in his face relaxing and a smile. Knew he was grateful that she wasn't probing.

'If you agreed, we would go to Mauritius and plan a small, low-key ceremony; lie low somewhere on the beach.'

Images streamed her mind: lying stretched out on golden sand, side by side with Logan, so close that if she reached out she'd be able to touch him. Long, cool drinks sipped by a

80   THEIR MAURITIUS WEDDING RUSE

pool. Walks through the fabulous scenery of
Mauritius; dinners for two at little local restaurants. Watching the sun set over a deep-
blue sea, turning to each other later in the
moonlight, tipping her face upwards and…

Jeez. Snap out of it.

What was wrong with her? That was not
a scenario that could play for her, not with
Logan, not with anyone. And she understood
that; she was good with that. Unfortunately
her hormones clearly weren't.

'It's up to you,' he said softly. 'And I would
fully understand if you decide to pull the rug.
I do understand what I am asking and, if it is
a lie too far, I will explain the truth to Belle.'

What to do, what to do? It was a lie of huge
magnitude and she knew the consequences of
lies; knew they could bring tragedy and death
in their wake. But this lie was the converse—
if she pulled the rug out, if she told the truth,
that truth could cause hurt and much more.
The truth would mean that Belle would have
to contend with the idea of Logan's deception,
and would have to face that her grandson was
not as settled and happy as she had believed.
There would be no wedding to plan, no reason to go to Mauritius.

How would that affect Belle's health and recovery? The changes Logan had described would be erased, and the impact could cause sadness, lower her resilience…and, God forbid, could even bring on another attack. If Belle didn't survive the operation, Chloe would have been the instrument of another tragedy. That was not acceptable—she would not let that happen.

'I'll do it.'

There was a pause and she saw the relief that etched his face as the tension in his shoulders eased. 'Thank you. I wish I could think of something more to say, to do. Please know that I truly appreciate your decision, from the bottom of my heart.'

There was no questioning his sincerity and she nodded. 'It's okay. I do understand why you want to do this.'

Then he smiled, a smile that rocked her. 'Belle was right about one thing: Mauritius is a truly beautiful place. Hopefully that will compensate a little.'

He moved closer and it dawned on her that with her decision the 'brief meeting' had now snowballed into a week in Mauritius of sun, sand and azure sea with this man: a man

82   THEIR MAURITIUS WEDDING RUSE

whose mere smile ratcheted her pulse; a man whom her feet were urging her to move towards. How on earth were they going to contain attraction in sun-soaked Mauritius?

'Plus,' he continued, 'Belle has agreed to retain your services. I will do the same. The holy grail may be a little closer.'

That was true, a fact Chloe latched onto. It was time to focus on facts. This would only be a few weeks of her life and a ceremony that would be cancelled out, a ceremony that would be kept private. No one need know. And when it was over she would be a rung higher on the career ladder. More importantly, she would have made sure history didn't repeat itself—she would not have caused more tragedy. That was what mattered most.

Attraction needed to be sidelined.

She nodded. 'You're right. Our priority for now is Belle and creating an illusion, but I won't lose sight of the holy grail. So...' She hesitated, feeling awkward. 'I know we discussed this earlier, but it is really important we keep things professional. When we're in Mauritius, I'll be bringing work with me and I think it's best we lie low as separately as possible.'

Even as she said the words Chloe felt regret start to surge as the barely formed images of lying on golden sand next to Logan dissipated.

Well, tough. It was the right call and it seemed as though Logan agreed.

'Absolutely,' he said. 'Neither of us wants to complicate the situation. I'll go back in and talk to Belle and then I'll check flight availability.'

An all too familiar hollow feeling descended in her tummy. Logan had said the flight was twelve hours long. Nerves began to twang and tighten even as she tried to tell herself it would be all right. That her fear of flying was under control. It was a fear more complex than her fear of cars, as it was a general fear, a knowledge that tragedy could happen—the idea that all the passengers surrounding her were at risk, and an irrational idea that perhaps she was a harbinger of doom. It all mixed up in her head, causing tautening, a throb and thrum of anxiety.

'You okay?'

'I'm fine.' She managed a smile and reminded herself that she did have strategies in place for when boarding a plane was unavoidable. 'Mauritius, here we come.'

84 THEIR MAURITIUS WEDDING RUSE

* * *

Twenty-four hours later, Logan glanced sideways at Chloe as they exited the airport and felt the warm glow of the Mauritius sun warm his shoulders through the cotton of his T-shirt. He glanced at Chloe, expecting to see her face relax into a smile, but instead a slight frown still creased her brow and strain lined her hazel eyes. Things he'd been aware of for the whole plane journey, alongside a look of worry, her fingertips kneading her temples, her body taut.

And who could blame her? He'd upended her life, pulled her away from an all-consuming job, and was expecting her to marry him, a man she'd met barely forty-eight hours before, in a country thousands of miles from home.

On top of that, she'd met with Belle yesterday. Whilst his grandmother had told him that he had chosen well, Chloe hadn't mentioned the meeting at all during the journey. In fact, she hadn't spoken at all, and he realised anew that he had put her in a difficult position, professionally and personally. Whilst he didn't, *couldn't*, regret what they were doing, his conscience panged. More so when he saw her footsteps drag a little as they approached the hire car and saw her hands clench over the seatbelt as he started the engine.

'Long flight,' he commented.

'Yes.'

'How about we stop *en route* to the villa? I don't know about you, but I'm cramped from sitting so long, and I'm hungry. We could stop to stretch our legs and grab some food?'

Her hand relaxed slightly. 'That sounds great.'

Half an hour later, he parked in a busy, bustling car park and they both climbed out of the car. She tipped her face up to the sun and rolled her shoulders as she inhaled the sea breeze coming in from the harbour.

'Could we stroll round the market?' she asked.

'Of course. We can get some street food from the stalls.'

They walked through the vibrant crowded streets towards the central market. 'Look out for the street art,' he advised. 'Local artists are commissioned or encouraged to paint murals, and there are so many to look at, tucked away in nooks and crannies throughout Port Louis.'

'When did you last come here?' she asked.

'About five years ago,' he said. 'When I was twenty-two.' The memory was a bitter one, the last time he'd seen his father. He'd asked Matt to come and had set the date three months after his actual birthday, a day his father never celebrated.

He'd explained once, 'I can't celebrate a day that is an anniversary of death, a reminder of all that I lost.'

Yet Logan had still hoped that maybe, now he was older, an adult, Matt would see him differently. That they could start to build a new relationship. It had been a vain hope. Matt had come to Mauritius but his visit had been insultingly brief. He'd spent exactly twenty-three minutes with his son, minutes in which he hadn't asked a single question about Logan's life, or about Belle.

He had answered questions monosyllabically and, after those twenty-three excruciating moments, he'd stood up and said, 'I'm sorry, Logan. This was a mistake. You and I…it can't work. Not right now.'

With that, he'd gone, and Logan hadn't seen

him since. He hadn't returned to Mauritius since either. Had never even told Belle about the whole incident.

'That's beautiful.' Chloe's voice pulled him to the present. She'd stopped in front of a vivid depiction of three women, arms round each other's waists, the art work strong and bold. 'It shows a sense of solidarity and constancy, and a mix of the ordinary and the extraordinary.'

She made an encompassing gesture. 'And all the other things as well. Did you see the landscapes? Leaves, fronds, lizards that look like they are really climbing... So much creative talent on display. It's wonderful that it's encouraged.'

Somehow seeing her enthusiasm, the glow in her eyes, made his own memories fade and made him appreciate anew the sheer vibrancy and harmony of the town where temples, mosques and churches all flourished.

'London feels like a long way away.' She shook her head. 'Well, obviously London is a long way away.'

'When is the last time you went on holiday?'

'Not for a while. It's never a good time, and I'd worry about getting behind.'

'They work you that hard?' he asked.

'Yes,' she said simply. 'But I knew it would be like that when I signed up.'

'And being a partner is worth that much to you.'

'Yes.'

'Why?'

There was a pause and when she met his gaze he saw a trace of defiance in her eyes, a challenge in the jut of her chin.

'Because I want to be the best. Corporate law is where the money is, where the success is, and being a partner is the pinnacle of that success.'

Somehow, though the words sounded stilted, almost rehearsed, and despite his knowledge of her credentials, they seemed at odds with Chloe herself.

Perhaps she read the doubt in his face. 'Don't you want to be the best at your job? Don't you get a kick when you bank another million?'

It was a fair question and he took his time before he answered it. 'I got a kick from the first million, but actually, no, I don't any more. To begin with it was important for me to stand on my own two feet.' Important, given that working for Belle's was an impossibility. Perhaps he would have worked that out for himself but his father had made it abundantly clear.

Matt's words to him were etched on his memory and his soul, divulged to nobody. 'You need to understand this, Logan—you can never be part of Belle's company. Never.'

Fourteen-year-old Logan had backed away as his father had leant down, in his face. 'If you do that, then it means you believe being heir apparent was worth your mother's death.'

And Logan had known there and then that he could never justify working for Belle's, however much he might have wanted to, so he'd worked out a way to earn his own living. Not mooch off Belle, as he knew his father did, though no one ever explicitly discussed it. But scraps of overheard conversation, and the fact his father never seemed to hold down a job, told its own story.

'I never set out to be a billionaire. I kind of fell into it. I mean, I always loved numbers—they speak to me. The patterns, the formulae, they work in my head. I always thought I'd be a maths professor or a teacher, and then one day my grandmother was talking about meeting her financial advisor about investments. I did some research and it all came together in my head, that numbers and money could be linked—real life and abstract. I used my pocket money and doubled it in hours.

'After that, I never really looked back. But it was more about the fun of it. I make money for myself and a select few clients. I have no wish to set up a global wealth-management business, or be one of the richest men in the world.'

'What will you do next?' she asked. 'Just keep adding to the bank balance?'

'I'm not sure. I don't need any more money in the bank. Hell, I don't need a fraction of what I've got. It's something I've been thinking about a lot. I fell into wealth management because my brain happens to be wired a certain way, but there's no merit in it.'

'There are different ways to achieve merit. If you wanted to, you could use your money philanthropically—set up foundations, charitable trusts... There are all sorts of ways you could do good with your wealth and still have plenty left. If you really meant it about retaining me, I could help with the legal side of that.'

'You sound like that's something you really believe in.'

'I do. I like the idea of using the law to do good.'

Logan could hear the sincerity in her voice, and the enthusiasm, and he wondered why she'd pursued corporate law, his curiosity well and truly piqued. Her whole face had lit up when she'd spoken about charitable foundations, about doing good, and somehow it was hard to equate that woman with a cutthroat corporate lawyer. Hard to reconcile the Chloe Edwards who had agreed to this whole plan, at considerable risk to her professional ambitions, with a cut-throat lawyer. On top of that, she was quite simply cut from a different cloth from the two other candidates he'd met with.

'Anyway, that's enough of me wittering on.'

'You aren't wittering.'

'I feel like I am. Shall we head for the market now?'

'Sure.' Sensing she was worried, that she'd revealed too much, he remained silent as they walked.

They approached the central market, and as they drew near the raucous sounds of the stall holders reached them, calling out about their wares, attracting and vying for the visitors' business. He led Chloe past the outlying stalls with their tourist merchandise and further inside to the area that sold local produce, a vibrant bustle of colour infused with the scent of ginger, lemon, chillies and a glorious array of spices and vanilla.

Glistening piles of chillies of all hues of green and red contrasted with the deep-purple mounds of aubergines and the knobbly roots of ginger, and above hung curved bunches of bananas in an array of vibrant yellow. Tropical fruit was arranged in tempting displays, mangos and papayas mixed with the earthy brown of coconuts.

'I've never seen or smelt anything like it.' Chloe turned to look at the spice stalls. Sacks of different powders tinged the air with tantalising aromas, and the vibrant red of the chili powder was set against the deeper red of pimento and the turmeric, and delicate saffron mingled with curry powder in different hues of yellow and browns.

Standing there looking at Chloe—at the tendrils of strawberry-blonde hair that had escaped from her ponytail to frame her face, her hazel eyes sparkling with interest and enthusiasm now, no longer holding the strain from earlier—it occurred to Logan that he'd never met anyone like Chloe. Had never felt this strange sense of connection, of trust. What other woman would have agreed to this masquerade without thought of payment? He couldn't think of any, and he vowed to make this time in Mauritius a break for Chloe to make up for the stress and pressure he'd put her under.

'What's up?' she asked, suddenly looking adorably self-conscious. 'Have I got turmeric on the end of my nose or something?'

'No. I was just thinking how…' *Beautiful you look.* He left the words unspoken, reminding himself that their relationship was professional and that it needed to stay that way. That was what Chloe wanted, and so did he. He couldn't risk complicating things, couldn't let emotions get in the way of Belle's well-being. He wasn't looking for a relationship, especially not one with someone who was already evoking unfamiliar sensations and emotions—an attraction that seemed to have a life of its own, impervious to an attempt to control it.

But it was more than that. Chloe evoked curiosity in him, questions about what made her tick, as well as an odd sense of protectiveness. All too much on any length of acquaintance, let alone a few days. He didn't want a relationship filled with emotions, or anything complicated, so he had no intention of starting anything.

He settled for, 'How hungry I am. How about we try some of the food?'

'Sounds good.' She smiled up at him. 'I'm in your hands. What would you suggest?'

'I think we should start with *dholl puris*.' He looked round and headed towards the food stalls, turned back and realised he couldn't see Chloe; the rush of shoppers had separated them. Then there she was, her face a little flushed and still so goddamned beautiful. He held out a hand, telling himself it made sense, that it was a practical measure so that they didn't lose each other in the crowds.

For a moment she hesitated and then he'd have sworn she heard him mutter, 'It makes sense.' She put her hand in his and— kaboom—there it was, that buzz, that thrill, that connection. But there could be no harm in it surely? Not in a crowded market place where they couldn't act on the 'kaboom' factor even if they wanted to. Which they didn't.

They stopped at a stall and minutes later were biting into the *puris*, a flat bread with a ladleful of spiced yellow lentil filling rolled into it. 'This is incredible,' Chloe said. 'There's cumin and turmeric, I think... I suddenly feel inspired to cook.' She grinned. 'Believe me, that doesn't happen very often, but I actually think I could eat these every day.'

'Now how about trying an *anana confit*? Chilli-salted pineapple.'

They stopped outside a stall and watched as the vendor expertly cut through a small miniature pineapple, leaving on the top, dunked it into a bag containing the coating and shook it vigorously, before handing it to Chloe.

Choe bit into it slightly gingerly and then her face lit up. 'It's perfect! Refreshing, sweet, salt and spice... I love it. In fact, could I have another...?'

Once they'd finished, she smiled up at him. 'Thank you. That was exactly what I needed—the food, the drink and stopping here.'

They started to walk back through the market. 'So you're feeling better?' he asked.

'Yes.' She pressed her lips together, and for a second there was anxiety on her face.

Again, Logan's conscience panged. 'How about we stop for a coffee before we continue the journey?' he suggested. 'There's something I want to say.'

CHAPTER SIX

SEATED AT AN outside table overlooking the harbour, Chloe gazed out at the vista, at the azure blue of the sea, the lazily waving fronds of the palm trees and the jutting peaks, troughs and domes of the buildings that fringed the view. Then she looked up at Logan as he returned to the table with the coffee. Wondered what he wanted to talk about.

She studied the broad contour of his hand around the coffee cup, remembering the strength and warmth of his fingers around hers as they'd walked around the market, and she was aware of a deep, burning wish that this time could be something it wasn't. That it could be a holiday, could be personal time that allowed attraction to have its way.

She was aware of a sudden hope that he felt the same, a hope she knew she had to blight. Because her professionalism meant everything to her—her job, her career, the holy grail of partnership.

And a golden rule of professionalism was not to get involved with a client. Especially not one who would help you up at least two rungs of the career ladder. She barely even knew Logan, and if things became complicated then he could withdraw his business. Then she would have made yet another misstep, another mistake. All for the sake of what—a kiss? A night together? She could never venture more with anyone. Ever.

'You said you wanted to talk?' she asked.

'Yes. I wanted to apologise.'

'For what?'

'I saw how anxious you were on the flight here and in the car afterwards and it made me realise just how much I have asked of you. Given your strong professional ethics, the meeting with my grandmother must have been difficult. On top of that, a couple of days ago you hadn't even met me, and now I've embroiled you in a web of deceit. Dragged you to a strange country to marry a stranger.'

His sincerity was evident and warmth touched her, along with surprise that he'd even spotted her anxieties.

'I embroiled myself,' she said. 'I made a choice. It was my decision to make; you didn't pressure me. So there is no need to apologise. My meeting with Belle was fine. I am confident I can keep the professional and personal lines unblurred.'

Though the meeting had raised questions in Chloe's mind. Questions Belle had made clear she didn't want asked, and questions she would not put to Logan. Such as, where were Logan's parents? Why wasn't Logan in line to inherit a share in Belle's company? Belle had made it plain she wanted to know the options open to her for her company, and had made it equally plain that leaving her shares, or control, to any family member was not one of those options.

Belle Jamieson was notoriously tight-lipped on her private life and Chloe had decided to respect that privacy. But she certainly didn't want Logan to feel that she had felt uncomfortable with Belle, because she hadn't. 'What you saw on the plane and in the car, it's nothing to do with you or the situation we're in.'

'What is it to do with?' His voice was gentle rather than prying and she sensed he genuinely wanted to know, needed to know, because he did genuinely feel bad. Chloe sipped her coffee and tried to decide what to do. She could stone-wall, but it didn't sit well with her that Logan should think she regretted her choice to help him, because she didn't.

'It's no big deal. I'm a nervous flyer, that's all. Then going from being enclosed in a large metal contraption in the sky to a small metal contraption on the ground got a bit much.' She shrugged. 'It's really no big deal.'

But she heard her voice hitch as images crowded in of her father's grey car colliding with the massive breadth of the oncoming lorry, the screech of breaks, the agonised shout of denial, her brother's body slamming forward... The scene she revisited time and again in nightmares. The last moments of the father and brother she'd loved so much.

'Chloe? It sounds like it is a big deal. I wish I'd known—maybe I could have helped.'

'There's nothing you could have done.' Her voice was low, vibrant with pain. She knew he deserved the facts, so he could understand that there *was* no help, so she kept her voice matter-of-fact, devoid of emotion, just like a lawyer stating a case.

'My father and brother died in a car accident. Ever since then, travelling in cars makes me anxious. For some reason, it's had a knock-on effect with planes.'

Opposite her, Logan stilled and then he rose, moved his chair closer to hers and put his arm round her shoulder, his proximity, his bulk and his warmth offering comfort she knew she didn't deserve.

'Jeez, Chloe, I am so very sorry. For your loss, for the pain and the grief.'

She tensed and then for a brief moment allowed her body to relax against his before pulling away, gently but with finality, her face remote when she turned to him. 'Thank you. But you see, a fear of flying isn't really that big a deal—not compared to losing your life. So, as I said, I'm fine. It's not something I usually talk about. I just didn't want you to feel my anxieties were your fault.'

She drained her coffee and glanced at her watch. 'Do you think we need to go?'

'Yes, we do,' Logan said, then briefly touched her hand. 'I understand the subject is closed, but thank you for telling me.'

To her relief, he didn't speak as they walked back to the car and she was grateful for the fact that he seemed to understand she had no wish to share any more, no wish to open herself up to sympathy or compassion. What she did want was to put the conversation behind them and focus on what they were here to do.

She watched as Logan put coordinates into his phone and started the car. 'So, where are we staying?' Chloe asked. 'You said it was a villa, but that's all I know.' She'd left all the arrangements to Logan and had spent the day before the flight catching up on work and accepting the congratulations from a senior partner on landing such a prestigious client.

'Actually, I'm not sure exactly where it is. Belle said she wanted it to be a surprise. I assume it will be similar to the villas we used to stay in when we came on holiday when I was a child. Maybe even one of the same ones. They were fantastic—large and sprawling, with comfy furniture, and right on the beach. My grandmother's friends would come and stay or visit, make amazing food and stay up laughing and talking, dancing on the sand in the evenings.'

'That sounds magical,' she said. It also sounded perfect for keeping the distance between them.

'We're nearly there now,' he said. 'I'm hoping the keys will be in a drop-box.' He pulled up. They climbed out and Chloe glanced round at the villas that overlooked the sweep of sands. She saw the door to one of them open and two women emerge, one looked to be somewhere in her fifties, the other older perhaps in her eighties, both beaming as they waved at Logan.

Surprise crossed Logan's face and then he smiled and waved back, turning hurriedly to Chloe. 'That's Celeste, Belle's best childhood friend, and the younger one is her daughter Marie. I didn't know Belle had contacted them, but I guess she decided the "no publicity" rule didn't apply to them.'

Chloe assimilated the information. 'So they probably know about the wedding, and will be reporting back to your grandmother in detail?'

'Yup.'

Chloe turned and smiled as the two women reached them. 'Surprise!' they chorused, and Logan stepped forward and enveloped each in a hug.

Then he stood back, and Chloe stepped forward, hand outstretched. She told herself she could do this. All she had to do was smile and be pleasant and, seeing their genuine happiness at seeing Logan, that wasn't hard.

'I'm Chloe. Logan only had a chance to tell me a little about you, but it is lovely to meet you.'

Both women took her hand in turn. 'It's lovely to meet you too. The woman who captured Logan's heart.'

Chloe turned and Logan stepped closer to her, triggering the familiar magnetic tug of awareness. Seeing Celeste's and Marie's eyes study them she leant into the attraction as he put his arm round her waist.

She felt the quiver of her body's response and in that moment she suddenly realised exactly what she had taken on, what *they* had taken on—because now she stood so close to him and the strength of his body pressed against hers, the heat of his fingers seeming to burn through the thin cotton of her dress. And she didn't want him to drop his hand, didn't want to move. But she knew she had to, and knew that, whilst the attraction was real, it couldn't be acted on.

'I hope you don't mind Belle telling us; she thought we could help with the wedding planning.'

Marie raised her hands. 'And, please, rest assured we understand you want to keep it small and private, and we get it. Belle needs minimum excitement, even of the good kind. We also want you to know that when Belle gets here we will be looking after her, and we will make sure she has everything she needs. But, first up, Belle asked us to find you a place to stay—'

Celeste broke in, 'Which is easy, because my Marie—' she gave her daughter a look of pride '—has her own business letting out villas.'

'And I have the perfect one. A cosy love nest where you can relax and plan your wedding, on your very own islet. It's linked to the mainland by a timber bridge, and I hope you'll love it. I'll be your housekeeper, so I'll check in daily, but otherwise you'll have the place to yourselves. Here are the keys; I'll let the two of you explore the property yourself and I'll be back in the evening to cook you a dinner you'll never forget.'

Glancing at Logan, Chloe could see he looked as shellshocked as she felt at the realisation they would be under far more scrutiny than either of them had anticipated. But that was hardly Celeste's or Marie's fault; it was another consequence of telling a lie on top of a lie: the web became more tangled. And that meant more of this—more proximity, more faking an attraction that was real. The idea dizzied her, unleashing equal panic and anticipation, greediness to enjoy the sensations evoked by his touch.

'I can't wait to see it,' Chloe said quickly. 'Thank you so much for going to all this trouble—we truly appreciate it.'

'We really do,' Logan said. 'This is exceptionally kind of you both.'

Logan accepted a set of keys and soon he and Chloe were back in the car.

'They really care about you,' Chloe said. 'And about Belle.' She glanced at him. 'Which is great. But…'

'It complicates things,' he said. 'We will be on show a lot more than I expected.'

Before she could reply, Logan drove across a narrow stone bridge and Chloe gave a small intake of breath.

'It's stunning.'

It truly was. The villa nestled on a sandy islet surrounded by the sparkling turquoise waters of a lagoon. A single-storey building made of natural materials and topped by a flat rattan roof, the structure stood inside a circular wall shaded and fringed by a circlet of evergreen trees.

'It's…like something out of a story.' A fairy story, the type of story she knew not to be true—a fictional, unrealistic set-up culminating in a rose-tinted, fuzzy, impossible-to-achieve happy ending. Real life was not a fairy story, yet… As she gazed at the villa, then looked at the man standing next to her for a poignant, unexpected moment, Chloe wished it was. Now a sense of anxiety threatened; illusion and reality, fact and fiction, were blurring.

'Is something wrong?'

'I…this…all of this… They've gone to so much trouble and it's not real. Why don't we tell Celeste and Marie the truth? They care about Belle, they'd understand.'

Logan considered the idea and then shook his head. 'Too risky. Celeste is Belle's best friend—she may feel the need to tell her. Plus, the more people who know, the more chance there is of Belle finding out. And it doesn't seem right to ask them to lie.'

'But it also doesn't seem right to be lying

to them. They have gone to so much effort.'
More lies, more consequences, people hurt.

'I know. But in this situation I don't think
we have any choice. Sometimes maybe it is
okay to lie. Because the truth could be hurt-
ful. I can think of truths I didn't want or need
to know.'

Was he right? A memory of her mother's
words hit her—the words of blame, the revelation of the brutal truth that she was held responsible for her father's and brother's deaths.
Would she have said those words in her
mother's place? 'There are some things that
shouldn't be said even if they are the truth,
some questions that should remain unasked
and not answered.'

'I agree,' he said softly, with a conviction
she knew instinctively was born of experience, a personal perspective. She realised he
too had been hurt by truth that shouldn't have
been told. 'But once they're said they have to
be accepted and dealt with.'

Her gaze flew to his, she saw understanding there and it felt natural to reach out and
take his hand in his, a brief gesture of solidarity. Something morphed into being, the un-
dercurrent flared into a jolt of awareness, and

her fingers curled round his hand, just as his fingers did the same, not wanting to break the connection. She was not even sure what the connection was, but she knew it was there, his touch sending a shiver of desire over her skin, her pulse rate soaring. They stood like that for a timeless moment and then she stepped backwards, unsure how to process the whirl of sensations.

She took a deep breath. 'You're right. I think it is better to keep the truth to ourselves for now, rather than put them in a difficult position.' After all, why make Celeste and Marie accomplices, complicit in a lie? She gestured to the front door. 'Shall we look around?'

Logan unlocked the front door, they entered and turned into a lounge area. A wall-to-wall sliding glass door showed a terraced area and showcased the view—a dazzling stretch of water, shades of aqua, teal, blue and turquoise overlapping towards the horizon to meet the azure skyline. The interior was full of natural colours, wicker and rattan, comfort and luxury combined.

'It's beautiful.' As she looked out at the view it was impossible not to let the fairy-tale illusion back in, to imagine sitting next to Logan on the terrace, walking to the beach hand in hand, lying on the sun-warmed sand, Logan rubbing oil onto her back…

Enough.

They headed to the kitchen next, all cool, white walls with simple prints and a state-of-the-art oven and fridge. Then they walked down a tiled corridor with whitewashed walls adorned with simply framed prints. Chloe exhaled a small sigh of relief—presumably there were at least two bedrooms.

She pushed open one door. 'Wow.' She took in the splendour of a bathroom complete with wet room, ornate mirrors and tiles, backed out, moved to the next door and opened it to reveal…

'It's another bathroom,' she said. They stood and stared inside, almost blankly, as they took in the Victorian bath tub, then they moved back into the corridor and both stared at the final door. A door that, illogically, she didn't want to open. Which was silly—after all, perhaps the door led to an annex or a suite of rooms.

'I guess we should open it,' Logan said and they stepped forward, reaching out at the same time. Their hands brushed and she'd have sworn she could see sparks combust as her nerves tightened. Somehow the door swung open and she couldn't help it: she gave a small gasp.

No annex. No suite. Instead, a single bedroom, a room that epitomised a love nest, providing another element of the fairy tale. Romance mixed with decadence. The luxurious king-sized bed was strewn with rose petals, with the peep of dark silken sheets under a sumptuous duvet and lusciously plump pillows. A large art deco mirror adorned one wall, the shuttered window on another allowing in a gentle breeze scented with the tang of the sea and sun-warmed air, along with motes of tropical greenery. A dresser held a bottle of champagne and a heart-shaped box of chocolates.

Emotions swirled in her, desire, yearning, that this tableau could be what it was supposed to be. That she, that they, could act out what the setting called for. That she could turn, walk towards Logan, stand on tip toe, kiss him and then lead him by the hand to the bed...

Chloe realised her feet were acting of their own accord and that she had turned towards him. Then he stepped towards her, she saw his eyes darken with desire and all she wanted to do was take that one final step, feel his lips on hers, touch and be touched.

But she mustn't. She knew she had to break the spell before it was too late; before this all-consuming desire, this fairy-tale villa, messed with her head and allowed her emotions and needs to govern what was right.

That was what sixteen-year-old Chloe had done, and that had ended in tragedy. That was what twenty-two-year-old Chloe had done with Mike, and that had ended in hurt and disappointment. She would not do that now, she would not jeopardise her professional status and would not risk letting desire confuse her, con her into making bad decisions or risk causing hurt to anyone. She stepped backwards, felt the back of her legs against the bed and then the door knocker pounded.

'That must be Celeste,' he said and she could hear both regret and relief in his voice. 'We'll figure this all out later.'

She nodded and followed him to the front door, trying to pull herself together, to get in role, managing a smile as Logan opened the door.

'Hello.' Celeste glanced at both of them. 'I hope you like the villa? We promised Belle we would do you proud.'

'And you have,' Logan said instantly.

'We love it,' Chloe echoed. No way would she let this woman down, not when she could see how much trouble she and her daughter had gone to.

'I'm glad, and you're going to love the meal Marie and I are going to prepare for you as well. But first…whilst we cook, I thought you may want to go down to the beach and watch the Sega dancing.' She turned to Chloe. 'And, in case you want to join in, I brought you this. Belle asked me to choose it for you.'

Chloe accepted the bag and looked inside.

'It's a dress,' Celeste explained. 'For the dance. Sega dancers wear bright colours and a dress that goes with the movement of the dance.'

'I… I'll go and try it on.' What else could she say?

Once in the bedroom, she pulled the dress out of the bag, the material a swirl and whirl of exotic colours with a long, flowy, swirly skirt and a matching sleeveless top that would definitely leave a section of her midriff bare.

Without giving herself time to think, she changed, and stared at her reflection. She looked...different, a far cry from a professional corporate lawyer. She looked like...the Chloe she could have been if tragedy hadn't struck.

The idea brought her up short, a sudden memory giving her a glimpse of the girl she had been before the tragedy. A girl who'd loved to dance, a girl who'd had ideas and plans to make a difference—to save the environment, to do something worthwhile, to become a social worker or a teacher. That was a Chloe she had buried deep down, a Chloe she could never now be. Her path was irrevocable now, a path towards success, a path to attain her brother's dream. The dream she had taken on, the dream she *had* to fulfil.

For a moment she was tempted to change the dress, to come up with some excuse to give Celeste. But that wouldn't be fair, and what excuse could there be? And it didn't matter. The dress was simply a costume, just like the jewel that glittered on her ring finger, something she was wearing for Belle's sake.

The thought reminded her of the card in the bag and its message.

Dear Chloe,
I hope you enjoy this. I have the feeling you don't have a lot of fun. Work is important but so is play... I speak from experience.
Belle

The words brought a sudden, unexpected sadness—it was true; fun wasn't a large part of her life. And, though she'd once loved dancing, that had been before the accident. But tonight was different. This wasn't her choice, this had been thrust upon her. Another glance at her reflection, at the bright colours and her bare shoulders, brought a sudden sparkle to her eyes. Maybe tonight it would be alright to dance.

Logan turned as Chloe re-entered the room and stilled as he took in her appearance. She looked stunning, standing in the doorway against the backdrop of the dusky evening. The dress was a mass of colours, bold greens and vibrant yellows, with some blue thrown in for good measure. The top exposed a tantalising line of midriff and the skirt accentuated the slenderness of her waist. Her hair fell in waves of strawberry-gold to her bare shoulders and Logan could only stand and stare, mesmerised by her beauty.

She tucked a tendril of hair behind her ear and gave a tentative smile, her hazel eyes holding a soupçon of doubt, as if she were a little off-kilter.

Celeste clapped her hands and said with delight, 'You look beautiful.'

Turning to Logan, she beamed. 'You definitely have to dance tonight.'

Then she turned back to Chloe. 'He's an excellent dancer, he has all the moves.' She made a shooing gesture with her hands. 'Now, off you go. Dinner will be an hour or so. I'll leave it all here ready to heat up when you return.'

'Thank you, Celeste,' Logan said, dropping a kiss on her cheek before heading towards Chloe, and five minutes later they were walking across the driveway and towards the path.

'You do look beautiful,' he said and heat touched her cheeks.

'I feel...strange. I mean, it's not the sort of thing I usually wear. And, as for dancing, I haven't danced in a long time.'

Perhaps he imagined it but he heard a wistfulness in her voice. 'Then maybe tonight is the night.'

And somehow, as they walked along the treelined road, the words took on a deeper meaning.

'Tell me about Sega music,' she said.

'It originated in Mauritius in the age of slavery and has evolved since then. The music is vibrant and soulful. Some of the traditional instruments include a drum called a *ravane*, a wooden hoop with a goat skin stretched over it, and maracas are used as well as a triangle—though nowadays more contemporary instruments are sometimes used as well. As for the beat, it catches you, and the dance kind of takes over.'

'You know a lot about it.'

'Celeste and Belle and their friends used to dance a lot on our holidays here. I guess that's why Belle wanted you to have a go.'

Chloe shook her head. 'I'm not sure if letting the dance take over is very me,' she said firmly. Almost too firmly. 'I'll definitely enjoy watching but I'm not intending to join in.'

They arrived at the beach and made their way across the still warm sand towards a

118 THEIR MAURITIUS WEDDING RUSE

crowd of people and the sound of laughter and instruments tuning up. A bar had been set up, with a glittering array of lights, noise and splashes of colour setting an arc on the golden sand.

When Logan came back holding two rum cocktails, Chloe stood, sandals discarded, watching the dancers congregate on the beach. Torches had been lit, and the firelight cast and spun light and shadow as they flickered and flared in the dusk, creating an atmosphere that seemed to crackle and fizz with promise. Even before he sipped the drink, Logan felt a strum of anticipation, a sense, a promise, of freedom.

Chloe turned as the music started playing, the beat gaining cadence and speed against the lap of the waves as the dancers began their movements, and the colours mingled and swirled into a tableau of vivid movement.

Hips swayed in time to the music, but now Logan stopped watching the performers, his attention captivated by Chloe, who stood entranced next to him. He could almost see the music call to her, as if the notes themselves danced and swayed across the sand, glinting towards her, and without even realising it she was moving, swaying, her hazel eyes rapt.

This was a different Chloe. It was as if she had been freed of a weight, as if the music had somehow allowed her to place it down.

Now he held out a hand as other spectators started to move forward. 'Come on,' he said.

After a fractional hesitation, she gave him a quick and sudden smile but, instead of taking his hand, she headed towards the stage, beckoning him forward, and he realised she'd already twigged the essence of the dance—the lure, the tantalisation, the temptation and promise of the dance between a couple.

As the beat of the music grew faster and faster, they both became lost in the music, backwards and forwards, the tease and chase of courtship in the flickering light of the fire, part of myriad sensations, their movements showing each other things they knew they couldn't say, things that crossed the professional line. But here in the language of the dance, amidst the crescendo and tempo of the instruments, they both whirled breathless and connected, mirroring desire and passion.

Until the music wound down, slowed and finally ended and the throng of dancers started

120 THEIR MAURITIUS WEDDING RUSE

to separate, couples with their arms round each other's waists or hand in hand as they headed back to the bar.

'Wow,' he said. 'If we're talking about moves, I think you've got them.'

'You weren't so bad yourself,' she said. 'I loved that, it was…liberating. Exhilarating. I haven't danced like that for a long time. Thank you.'

She stood, flushed and breathless, and so undeniably beautiful that Logan's heart twisted as their gazes locked. All he wanted to do was pull her into his arms and kiss her. He tried to remind himself of the need to keep things professional, that succumbing to attraction could complicate the situation and backfire in a way that could harm Belle. But in truth it wasn't that which stopped him, it was fear. A realisation he'd never felt like this before.

Of course, he'd felt desire, attraction for other women, but this transcended that, and it scared him. Perhaps this was how his parents had felt for each other, and he never wanted to risk that sort of feeling, that depth of it. Because he'd seen what it led to if lost—a grief so profound that it could turn a person

NINA MILNE   121

against their own child. Could blight their
life. Could cause them to hurt others, as his
father had hurt Belle, had hurt Logan. Could
derail them. Logan had no intention of hurting anyone and had no intention of being derailed.

But that was how he felt now—derailed.
So instead of kissing her he stepped back,
smiled, cleared his throat and forced himself
to look at his watch. 'We'd better head back
to the villa.'

CHAPTER SEVEN

As THEY APPROACHED the villa, Chloe glanced sideways at Logan and wondered if he had any idea of the feelings, the need, churning inside her. She suspected that he did and that, if she had so much as inched towards him when the dance had finished, he would have made good on all the unspoken promises. And she'd wanted to; she'd wanted to so much that it had been a physical ache inside her, a yearning she knew only Logan could assuage.

But she had stayed rooted to the spot, frozen by fear. Because she hadn't recognised the woman she'd been, barefoot on the sand, lost to the beat of the music, caught up completely in the sensations, the exhilaration of the dance. But it hadn't only been about the dance, it had been about the man she'd been dancing with.

And that was a terrifying thought. Because suddenly she'd realised what she was scared of: herself. She was too reminiscent of sixteen-year-old Chloe, caught up in her own desires and needs, the Chloe who had loved dancing, the Chloe who had thought of herself as a free spirit. And she didn't want to be that person any more. Couldn't risk it. Couldn't afford it. That Chloe had brought chaos, and she'd worked so hard to erase her. She'd worked so hard for her professionalism, her status, her dream. Her brother's dream, her mother's approbation. Redemption.

That couldn't be thrown away, undone by her desire for one man. So she'd been careful to walk home at a distance, and only turned to him as they entered the house, inhaled the tantalising aroma of spices and saw Celeste's note with reheating instructions.

'I'll just quickly shower and change,' she said.

Maybe that would bring real Chloe back, she thought ten minutes later as she looked at the contents of her suitcase, at her own clothes, the outfits that showed who she was now. She chose a simple grey dress, way more in keeping with a professional image, something she would wear for dinner with a client. But somehow it didn't work; the dress was a veneer that couldn't suppress the tug and yearning of frustrated desire.

Chloe turned and headed for the kitchen. It would all wear off, she told herself, But the bubbling, churning sensations still roiled as she entered the room, and her treacherous pulse rate ratcheted as Logan turned away from the stove and smiled at her.

'Hey,' he said and she gulped, crossing one arm across her midriff in an attempt at defence against his sheer desirability, ridiculously aware of the strength and bulk of his body, the flow and hardness of muscle sending a tingle through her. He'd showered and changed as well, his dark shirt rolled up at the sleeves, the top button undone to reveal a tantalising triangle of flesh.

'You…it…something smells amazing.'

'It could be me,' he said and grinned, his brown eyes alight with a teasing light. 'I found a pretty incredible array of soaps in the bathroom.'

For a mad moment Chloe wanted to volunteer to move closer, bury her face in his neck and check it out.

'But I think it's more likely to be the food,' he continued, gesturing at the hob. 'Celeste has made *carri poisson*. It's a fish curry made with locally caught fresh fish and lots of spices—ginger, coriander, curry leaves, turmeric, thyme and cumin, to name but a few, according to her note.'

'That sounds incredible.'

'To be served with rice and rotis. She has also left chilled champagne and some snacks.'

He moved away from the stove and over to a cooler that held a bottle of champagne. A muted pop later, he poured the bubbling liquid into two crystal flutes and handed her one.

'To you,' he said, and Chloe shook her head, needing to remind them both why they were here.

'To Belle,' she said, and he nodded.

'To Belle.'

They clinked glasses and he smiled at her. It was a slow smile as he looked at her and the grey dress no longer felt like a safe veneer, a protection to deflect attraction. 'You still look beautiful,' he said simply and the words heated her skin.

'Thank you,' she said, and she couldn't help

126   THEIR MAURITIUS WEDDING RUSE

but smile back. Distracted herself by taking one of the snacks Celeste had left.

'This is amazing,' she said, needing to make conversation. 'What is it?'

'A *gato arouille*. You grate taro roots and deep-fry them till they're crisp.'

'They're salty and sweet. I could eat these every day, followed by the pineapples.'

'Wait till you taste the main course. Celeste has set us a table outside, so we can take it straight out there.'

They walked outside and down the wooden steps that led to the beach and Chloe gave a small gasp of delight. 'It's magical.'

A beautifully laid table was set on the sand, complete with crystal glasses, linen napkins and gleaming cutlery. A single flower gave a vivid burst of colour as the centrepiece. The table itself was illuminated by a heart-shaped trail of fairy lights that lit up the sand and showed the dark-blue lap of the waves, crested by the glow of the iridescent moon.

And now, however hard she tried, it was harder and harder to see this as a prop, a scene set in belief in a fake relationship. It didn't feel fake, not when he stood so close she could catch the scent of the soap; so close that her whole body was alert and desperate to close the gap, to shift a little bit closer.

'Perhaps we should send a photo to Belle.' Her voice was shaky.

'Good idea.' Logan took his phone from his pocket and turned to her. 'Ready?' he asked and his voice was smooth and deep. Somehow the question felt significant.

'Sure,' she said, her voice breathless, and they both looked at the camera and smiled.

'There we go,' he said. They looked at the image together and she caught her breath. She looked different, a far cry from the woman who'd so blithely greeted Logan a few days before in her office. And he looked different too; she could see warmth and desire in his eyes, captured in that single instant.

Chloe pressed her lips together, knowing she—they—had to refocus on reality, and she forced herself to walk away, sit down at the table and make conversation.

'This must have been an amazing place for Belle to grow up in—I can see why she wants to come back, and why she wants you to get married here.'

'She's always loved it. This is the place where her interest, her fascination, with cosmetics began, and where she met and married her first husband—Bertrand Escalier. The one she describes as the love of her life.'

'What happened?'

'She said it was a time before "new men", a time when a "real" man provided for his wife and family. Or at least, that was what he believed. And she believed in their love so deeply that she underestimated that belief. In the end, he couldn't cope with her success, and by then she was too hooked to give it up. But I think it's a decision she regrets to this day.'

Chloe sipped her drink and looked out. 'I wonder what that feels like. To regret that sort of achievement. I wonder if he regrets letting her go.'

Logan shrugged. 'After the divorce, she never contacted him again. They didn't have children and they'd moved away from Mauritius by then. I don't know if he came back. Belle married twice more but neither marriage worked out. My grandfather was husband number three but they split when Belle was pregnant with my dad, and he was never part of their lives. Maybe that's why I'm not a big believer in love. I mean, the real thing didn't work out, and neither did the second chances. It seems like it's not really worth the risk.'

Studying his face, Chloe wondered if that was the real reason and sensed there was something more. 'Is that how you see love? As a risk?'

'Sure. You risk your heart, you risk pain, you risk hurt, you risk loss. And against that is the chance of finding "love"—riding a roller-coaster of highs where your heart is at risk every single day. Belle tried to explain it to me, how she felt about Bertrand—the intensity, the depth, the passion and then the deep, deep hurt and betrayal. I don't think the highs are worth the risk of the lows. I'm more of an even-keel sort of guy.'

He sounded certain, his voice that of a man who had come to a definitive decision he would stand by.

'Have you ever been in love, in a long-term relationship?'

'Nope and I have no intention of ever doing so.'

'But how would you stop yourself?'

'Shut the relationship down at the first sight of love on either side. It's like pulling out of

130   THEIR MAURITIUS WEDDING RUSE

an investment, selling at the right moment before you lose anything.'

'But how do you identify that moment?' God knew, she hadn't with Mike. And by letting the relationship run on she'd raised hopes of marriage in Mike's heart. She'd caused hurt and pain. Not intentionally, but that didn't make it any better.

'I'm always clear going in that I'm not interested in marriage or a long-term commitment. I tend to date women who feel the same way I do. They're not looking for that either, for whatever reason. My last relationship was with a recent divorcee; she'd come out of a marriage and she just wanted someone to have fun with, someone who would care, but nothing heavy—liking, respect and a spark.'

'What happened?'

'After about eight months it fizzled out, which suited us both. That was eighteen months ago and I haven't dated seriously since.'

'But you didn't love her?'

'Nope. I cared about her, I wanted her to be happy—I still do. I enjoyed the time we spent together. That's a type of love, I suppose. But not the roller-coaster sort of love where your whole being is caught up in the other person.'

'Where you care enough that it matters if you lose them? Where your happiness depends on them and vice versa?'

'That's it exactly. I like my relationships to not be all-consuming. But whilst I'm with someone I believe in fidelity and trust.' He glanced across at her. 'What about you?'

'I told you. My holy grail is partnership. It's all about work. I have no interest in any type of relationship.'

'Your career is more important than a personal life?' he asked.

'Yes.' It seemed important to remember that, to state the fact, sitting here looking out over the glimmering dark sea, at the bubbles of the champagne glittering and popping in the flickering candlelight, at the canopy of stars overhead.

Most magical of all was the proximity of Logan. His dark-brown eyes were intent on her, making her feel as if she mattered, as if what she said was of interest. 'I'm in control of my career. If I mess it up, it's on me. A personal relationship—it's not under my control. I'd rather pass.'

That was true, but there was more to it than that. She'd learnt that relationships led to a possibility of inflicting hurt, and she'd done enough of that in her life. Worse, any relationship she now had would raise hopes in her mother that a grandson might be possible and Chloe felt a tug of sadness—how could she have a child to please her mother? Especially when the idea terrified her. How could she be trusted to care for a child, she who had already brought tragedy to those she loved best?

She blinked the thoughts away. She'd made her peace with her decisions: no more relationships.

'For ever?' he asked. 'All relationships? Isn't that a bit extreme at twenty-six?'

'You've vetoed love and marriage aged twenty-seven.'

'Sure. But I'm not planning a life of celibacy. But there's more than that. My relationships are about companionship, enjoyment, laughter, fun...' His voice deepened. 'In bed and out.'

Chloe was mesmerised; it almost felt as though that was on offer here. She blinked the thought away, refusing even to let herself follow that thought or allow herself even to imagine the scenario.

'I wouldn't want to give up that aspect of my life.'

'It's not that easy.'

'Why not?' he asked. 'I'm managing fine. Unless—and there is nothing wrong with this—if you're looking for love and the real thing, then don't rule it out. It is possible to have a career and a successful marriage.'

Chloe shook her head. 'I don't want marriage. But I also have no idea how to manage a relationship like you do.'

He narrowed his eyes. 'Have you tried?' he asked. 'Have you ever been in love?'

Chloe shook her head and felt the familiar sense of perplexion, almost embarrassment along with the all too familiar sense of guilt at her own actions. 'No.'

He reached out and placed his hand over hers briefly. 'Want to talk about it?' he asked. 'I won't judge. Hell, I have no right. I'm pretty sure there would be plenty to judge my take.'

'Not me,' Chloe said. 'I think I may envy it.' She thought about taking him up on his offer, thought about talking about it, and re-alised to her own surprise that she wanted to.

Logan did seem to have figured it out, he had a different take, though he shared the same disbelief in the power of love.

'At least you've worked out a way to have a relationship. I haven't, and when I tried it went really wrong.' She sipped her drink. 'I met Mike when I was twenty-two. He was twenty-six and he was an accountant. Similar to me in lots of ways with the same ambitions. He seemed ideal. Everyone said what a wonderful couple we made. But…'

He waited but didn't prompt her, giving her time, and she continued.

'But it didn't progress. I thought we'd fall in love, but *I* didn't. However hard I tried, I could see his good points, but I couldn't feel them. I tried everything—supported his football team, cooked his favourite foods, encouraged his dreams. I kept telling myself to give it time, that I was over-thinking. That we were doing okay, our relationship was taking its own path, he felt the same as me…blah blah. And then out of the blue he suggested we move in together. He mentioned marriage, said he loved me.'

She could hear the shock, the disbelief, in her voice now as she remembered. 'But of course I couldn't marry him, not when I didn't love him.' Because she never could; love was outside her remit. 'It was pretty awful. He was furious. He said I'd regret it, that I'd led him on…'

Chloe recalled the scene, the phrases and insults he'd hurled at her. 'It doesn't matter what he said, he had every right to be angry.'

Logan frowned. 'I disagree. I would feel compassion for him if he'd been devastated, been truly heartbroken. But it sounds to me as though his pride was hurt, not his heart. Either way, it's not your fault you didn't love him, and it certainly doesn't mean you couldn't love somebody else.'

Chloe shook her head. She knew she wouldn't, but couldn't explain the full truth to him, the impossibility of love for her. 'I don't want to navigate another relationship, hurt or be hurt. I'd rather get on with my life and be responsible for my own happiness, be able to focus on what's important to me. I don't want the emotions and minefields that come with the possibility of love. It's all too complicated, too much, too out of control with no guarantees.'

'I agree with all of that, but don't be too hard on yourself. Mike sounds like someone who looks good on paper but didn't measure up in real life. Like the other solicitors I met with—great CVs but they weren't right for my grandmother.'

'Then I shouldn't have kept dating him.'

'I guess you kept hoping he'd change.'

'I think I kept waiting for me to change.'

Logan reached out and covered her hand in his, the warmth, the comfort, instant. 'You don't need to change. You are a smart, beautiful, kind person.'

There was no mistaking his sincerity as his clasp tightened, giving depth and reassurance to the words.

'Thank you,' she said.

'It's the truth. And for what it's worth I don't think you should give up on all relationships just because of one failed one. Better to learn from it. If you truly don't want love, that's fine, but it doesn't mean you should give up on companionship, attraction, fun and enjoying spending time with a partner in a temporary relationship.'

She looked at him and felt a sudden flutter, a thrill, and it was as if it was someone else's voice and not her own that spoke. 'Is that an offer?'

'Do you want it to be?' His voice was low and deep, and now her skin shivered despite the warmth of the night. He rose to his feet, his dark-brown eyes mesmerising, dark with desire he made no effort to hide. 'Whilst you think about it, would you like to dance? Marie has set up a record player with records.'

Dance with Logan…just the two of them on this stretch of sand, the starlight pinpoints of faraway illumination, with the salty tang of the dark-blue waves dappled in moonlight? Feel his arms around her this time and be able to touch, to be pressed against the muscular lithe strength of his body…?

Common sense dictated she refuse but she couldn't. It was as simple as that. The thought of denying herself this was an impossibility. She told herself that it was only a few minutes, a few magical moments, and then she would return the status quo to professionalism.

But then she put her hand in his, heard the haunting song of a long-dead jazz singer weave magic in the balmy, moonlit night air as the notes of the saxophone segued with the gentle lap of the water and Logan's large hands enclosed her waist, seeming to brand her, heat her through the thin material of her dress. Her hands landed on his chest and she could feel the beat of his heart.

Then they were lost in the sheer wonder of proximity as she revelled in his closeness, the swell of hard muscle, his thigh against hers. As the last swirl of notes resonated and floated around them, they came to a stop, his hands still spanning her waist. As she looked up at him, the moonlight glinting highlights in his blond hair, his brown eyes dark with desire, serious and questioning, she gave him the only possible answer—she stood on tip toe and brushed his lips with her own.

Then his lips were on hers and it felt so right that she knew resistance was an impossibility, that this was inevitable and infinitely desirable. She was lost in a world, a universe, of sensation as the earth seemed to tilt on its axis, leaving only this—the feel, the taste of him. She pressed closer, looped her arms round his neck and revelled in the glorious texture of his lips as he deepened the kiss. She heard a gasp, but had no clue whether it was Logan or herself, and it didn't matter, because in this moment they were as one, locked in a vortex of sensation.

She felt his smile, and any and all rational thoughts went flying as she gloried in the rush of exquisite, visceral reality of a kiss that dizzied her, sent liquid heat through her and left her wanting, yearning, needing more.

The crackle of the record broke the spell and they moved apart and stood staring at each other. Then he moved to lift the needle and turned back to her, and there was no need for words.

There was no room for anything other than sating the urgency of desire. He reached out for her hand and then they were walking, then running, back to the house, through the living room, down the corridor and into the bedroom, where the rose-strewn bed awaited.

CHAPTER EIGHT

LOGAN OPENED HIS EYES, aware of a languorous sense of contentment and felt his face stretch into a smile as he recalled the past hours. He shifted slightly so he could see Chloe still asleep beside him, her glorious hair a halo on the pillow, one hand resting lightly on his chest, the touch reassuring and sweetly sensual.

Yet as he lay there he could feel a small, nagging worry surface, a realisation that last night he'd given no thought to anything but Chloe, and had in fact been railroaded by desire, by a sense of connection. By the impossibility of doing anything other than he had done.

She stirred now, opened her eyes and regarded him sleepily. Then he saw recollection dawn and sleep evacuated the hazel eyes, replaced by a slight wariness, and she moved away, holding the duvet close to her as she sat up, not leaving the bed but poised and ready to do so.

'Morning,' he said, keeping his voice light as he smiled at her. A smile she returned, but it was a perfunctory one, and he could see thoughts chase themselves across her face.

'Morning,' she said. She glanced towards the window and then at her watch. 'It's nine o'clock,' she said. 'Marie or Celeste may arrive any minute. May even be here now. We should get up.'

'I imagine they've already been and gone. Even if they are here they won't mind if we're not up.'

'Still. It's late and we have things to do and...'

'And you're regretting last night?' he asked. He tried to keep his voice even; that was her prerogative, as no promises had been made. Yet the idea caused a pang of hurt in his gut, but also a desire to shield her from regret, from sadness.

'No...yes... I don't know. I'm feeling a little...conflicted. And awkward. And...'

'Don't feel awkward,' he said. He didn't want her to feel that. 'What happened last night was incredible and natural and magical. For me anyway.'

He saw her relax slightly, though her grip on the duvet was as fierce as ever.

Then she nodded. 'It was all those things, but it still shouldn't have happened. We agreed that we would keep things professional.'

He could hear the self-censure in her voice, and understood how important her career, her professionalism, were to her. But he sensed it might go even deeper than that.

'I get that. But…perhaps we were a little optimistic.' He shifted up the bed so that he too was against the headboard, careful not to edge too close to her. 'The attraction has been there from the get-go. And our fake engagement is forcing us into a proximity that makes fighting the attraction way harder than it would have been normally. So perhaps last night was inevitable, but whether it was or not, we can't change it. As for now, for the future…that's up to us. But, whatever we decide, I know I have no regrets, and even if I could turn the clock back I wouldn't change a single minute.'

How could he want to erase the evening, or the night that had followed—the laughter, passion, gentleness and urgency? The give and take of glorious, exquisite reciprocal pleasure? The scent of her, the taste of her, the tickle of her hair on his chest whilst she slept?

Chloe gave a small smile but worry still flecked the hazel eyes. 'Thank you,' she said. 'But boundaries are there for a reason.'

'Sure. But sometimes boundaries need to be renegotiated. Last night we crossed the line, but now we decide if we want to redraw them or cross back. No harm, no foul.'

'No harm, no foul,' she repeated and gave a small nod. 'Would you mind if we discussed the boundary situation over coffee?' She gave a small smile. 'And with our clothes on.'

'No problem.' He swung his legs out of bed and kept his back to her as he wriggled into his discarded jeans from the night before and rose. 'I'll go use the bathroom and I'll see you in the kitchen,' he said.

'Thank you. I won't be long.'

As he left the room, Logan was aware of edginess, hope that Chloe would decide to continue what they'd started, alongside knowledge that perhaps it made more sense for her not to. He'd spoken the truth—he couldn't regret the previous night—but he couldn't ignore the fact that this transcended his previous forays into relationships. The attraction fiercer, the connection stronger, a sense that he was on the up of a roller-coaster and the only way forward at some point would be down.

But...the idea of stopping now was not one he wanted to think about either. His mind whirled, calculating risks, probabilities. He told himself this was a safe bet, because neither of them had any interest in anything long-term. So perhaps there was a way to bring the roller-coaster onto the level, where there was no danger of things getting out of hand, no risk of complicated emotions plunging the carriage down.

Half an hour later, Chloe felt at least a little more herself, a little more in control, though she couldn't help but let images from the previous night run through her mind. She marvelled at her own lack of inhibition, at how she and Logan had connected and had been able to give and receive pleasure beyond her wildest imagination. Her whole body had been aching, sated and yet ready for more.

That was the question, wasn't it? Could

there be more? More nights like the previous one? But more nights could lead to more feelings, more emotions… Already she felt consumed by a sense of exhilaration and sensed a growing connection, the type of minefield she'd vowed to avoid. Yet, how could she resist?

She entered the kitchen to find the table set and Logan standing at the coffee machine. Her tummy did a soar and dip.

'Marie or Celeste have been in. They've left fresh baguettes and Celeste's signature dish to put in them: *gateaux piments*, loosely translated as "chilli cakes". They're made from chana dal and Celeste's secret ingredients, then deep fried. She's also left a note with a few recommendations of places to shop for wedding things and places for us to check out as a venue.'

Surely Logan was talking a little faster than usual, was a little less assured? Could it be that he too didn't know what to do for the best? Was he working out if this relationship was a viable emotional investment?

'But, before we plan the day and where we'll go first, I guess we should talk about boundaries.'

Chloe nodded, sat down and smiled her thanks as Logan poured her coffee and pushed across a jug of milk. 'What do you want to do?' she asked.

'You already know how I run relationships. I'd like us to spend some time together—keep professional and personal separate—but I understand that may not work for you.'

Disproportionate happiness that he wanted to spend more time with her, wanted to extend the relationship, fizzed through her and she couldn't help the smile that touched her lips. He wanted liking, respect, a spark, fun in bed and out and, damn it she wanted that too.

But… 'You said that your relationships were elastic timewise, that they fizzled out or came to natural ends. That wouldn't work for me.'

Logan had said he'd get out at the first sign of the emotional investment becoming too much—how would she know when that point came? The idea of always watching for signs in him, and in herself, that she knew she wouldn't be able to read sent waves of anxiety through her. But it wasn't just that—Chloe wouldn't raise hopes in her mother's heart again, hopes that had no chance of fulfilment.

'It would make our professional relationship too complicated, the lines too blurred.'

'So what do you want to do?' His voice was even, with no hint of any pressure, but she could see a slight tension in his jaw and in the curl of his fingers around his mug. For an instant her eyes focused on his hand and recalled the touch of those fingers on her.

He waited her answer, his brown eyes steady. Her head told her to call it here and now. Her body said something different as she recalled his touch, the way he'd listened to her, the warmth of his body and the warmth of his words.

'I think we have to be realistic,' she said. 'I could sit here and vow to keep it professional. I could build a wall of pillows between us in the bed, or sleep on the sofa, whatever. But I don't think it would work.' She huffed out a sigh. 'I suspect I would climb over the barrier in my sleep.'

'And I think I'd sleepwalk to the sofa and carry you back to bed, caveman-style.'

'Then I suggest we put a time limit on this. We keep this relationship going until we tell Belle the truth. After that, we revert to the professional boundaries. What do you think?'

Chloe examined her idea as she waited for Logan to consider it. Surely that would be pretty water-tight? Her mother need never know anything about a relationship with Logan. No one would get hurt. She couldn't hurt Logan; he had the avoidance of love down to a fine art, and had weathered relationships for months without succumbing. As for herself, she'd been with Mike two years, desperately trying to fall in love with no result, so she was clearly immune, especially over such a short time span.

This would be a temporary fling in forced proximity, within a fake relationship. Then they would redraw the professional lines in indelible ink. It all made sense. And, if a small bell clanged a warning at the back of her head, Chloe chose to ignore it.

'That sounds good to me.' Logan rose to his feet and grinned at her. 'And now...' He approached her and, before she realised his intention, she found herself slung over his shoulder. 'Now I'm taking you back to bed.'

An hour later they returned to the breakfast table and Chloe grinned at him. 'I think I may be able to manage a second breakfast.'

'I think we've burned up enough calories to warrant at least three more breakfasts.' He picked up his phone from the table as he spoke and his expression changed. Shock, frustration and then a frown furrowed his brow.

'What's wrong? Is it Belle?' The idea that something had gone wrong was unthinkable.

'It's not Belle.' His voice was curt. 'Excuse me.' With that, he turned and walked from the room, phone to his ear, without any further explanation.

Chloe gazed after him, anxiety churning in her stomach. Something had clearly gone wrong and, irrationally, she had the feeling it was somehow her fault. She told herself not to be foolish. If something bad had happened whilst they'd been in bed, that could not conceivably be down to her.

Yet…it felt as if it were. Anxiety churned in her tummy as she stared at the table and started clearing things away, her appetite suddenly gone. Once the kitchen was pristine she set up her laptop in the living room, and had just completed the report she'd promised to send Belle after their meeting when Logan returned, his face closed, lips set in a grim line, though he attempted a smile.

150   THEIR MAURITIUS WEDDING RUSE

'Sorry. That took longer than I thought. We'd better get going. I suggest we divide up some tasks on the list. I need to get the legal stuff sorted, though I have managed to expedite a licence due to Belle's condition. I'll also check out a couple of possible venues. You could check out the others and we can compare notes this evening.'

Chloe opened her mouth and closed it again. Logan's voice was curt, perfunctory, a far cry from that of the man who had carried her to bed over his shoulder, the man who, once there, had given her such glorious pleasure.

Was it *because* they'd been to bed? She had no idea. She already didn't get the rules, didn't understand what was going on. But she'd be damned if she asked or showed any sense of pique or disappointment. 'Sure. That sounds like a plan. I'll have a look for a dress as well.'

She tried to tell herself this was no big deal. That, given the time constraints, it made sense for them to split up for the day.

Yet it did matter. Because this was further proof that she'd read the signs wrong. Just as she had with Mike—she hadn't realised he loved her, hadn't understood her mother wanted a grandson. And now she'd believed that Logan might want to spend the day with her. She'd been sure of it, in fact. Of course, it could be he'd changed his mind because of whatever he'd seen on his phone. Something he clearly had no intention of sharing, and that hurt too.

God, she hated this, this sense of uncertainty. *Enough.* She was not going to let one night—well, one night and one morning—of spectacular sex turn her into a mess. That would be ludicrous. She was more than capable of having a lovely day on her own in a place as beautiful as Mauritius. She did not need her hand held by Logan, or anyone. The thought stiffened her spine and she smiled easily at him.

'That works.'

'Okay. Let's go. We can decide who is going where in the car.'

He glanced back down at his phone as it beeped, his expression unreadable once more.

It remained unreadable for the car journey. And, once they had gone their separate ways, despite the beauty and vibrancy of Mauritius her thoughts strayed to Logan way too much and she knew that had to stop. They were here to plan a wedding and their temporary relationship was of secondary importance. Soon enough they would be nothing more than professionals, client and lawyer. That was the long game. So tonight she would make sure to set a businesslike tone—no more dancing on the sand.

CHAPTER NINE

LOGAN APPROACHED THE restaurant Chloe had chosen, a glorious tranquil outdoor space in a lush forest area of the island. Picnic-style tables were dotted around and the verdant trees were wreathed with fairy lights that twinkled and illuminated the dusky evening. The smoky, tantalising aromas of barbecue tinged the air but it wasn't the food or setting that Logan was thinking about. It was Chloe.

He slowed his steps, reminding himself of the need to pull back. He'd been so caught up in Chloe that he'd messed up, big-time. For the first time since Belle's heart attack, he'd left his phone out of arm's reach, out of hearing range. And as a result he'd missed his dad's call.

Anger at himself rekindled and he took a deep breath. He'd fix this, even if he wasn't sure how. He had no idea what to do next to find Matt. But he did know he had to take a step back from Chloe. He still couldn't fathom that he'd been so caught up in her that he had made such a fundamental error.

He walked towards the table, set under the spread of a banyan tree, and there was Chloe. Despite his resolve, a sudden warmth bathed his chest along with that instant tug of desire as she rose to her feet, stood in the dappled shade of the trees with her back straight, the epitome of grace, the sun dress covered by an elegant shawl.

Her lips upturned in a smile, but it was a smile that held a wariness, a reticence that was echoed in her hazel eyes, and perhaps mirrored in his own. 'Hi. I hope this is alright. We had dinner on a beach last night, so I thought we could eat in a different setting today. I called Celeste and she suggested this place.'

'This looks great,' he said, as the waiter materialised and handed over the menus. He looked down at the choices. 'Really great,' he added even though he wondered if Chloe had wanted to avoid the complete privacy of eating at the villa, and if this was a signal that she too wanted to pull back.

'I know, right? I got here early so I'd have time to decide what to eat. It always takes me at least ten minutes and I didn't want to waste time. I know we need to discuss the wedding plans.'

Her tone was a mix of friendliness and business-like. 'I've narrowed it down to two choices. There's a fish dish where they marinate a fish called a bomli in mustard seeds, vinegar and other spices, served with a chilli nut chutney, traditional fried potatoes and rice cooked with tomato and thyme. Or I could have a lamb curry cooked with butter beans and something called "suran".'

'It's a type of yam, so a bit like sweet potato, only I think it's a bit nuttier in taste.'

'That sounds lovely, and it's served with a squash fricassee, papaya salad and a flatbread called a *faratha*.' She sighed. 'So how on earth do I decide?'

'Easy. We order both and share.'

'Perfect. Thank you,' she said, as the waiter returned and took their orders. 'So,' she said. 'I've had some ideas about the wedding.'

'Go ahead.'

'I went to the hotels and, whilst they are all fabulous, I've come up with what I think may be a better idea. Especially because we want to make this as stress-free and calm for Belle as possible. And minimise any chance of any publicity.'

'Agreed.' He might not be in the public eye but Belle was.

'Why don't we ask Celeste and Marie to find a villa? One with enough room for Belle and her medical team. She can come straight there and then the next day we can hold the ceremony at the villa itself—in the garden or on the beach, depending on where it's located. Celeste and Marie can be witnesses. Then we can have some food afterwards. That should hopefully not be too much for Belle. What do you think?' Her face held enthusiasm, the earlier wariness gone.

'I think that's a brilliant idea. I'll discuss it with Marie first thing tomorrow.'

He sat back as the waiter arrived with the food and for a while they busied themselves with serving themselves. Then Chloe took a deep breath.

'How was your day?' she asked.

'Fine,' he said quickly, too quickly. 'I sorted out the licence and spoke to a celebrant, so the ceremony is now officially going ahead.'

'Great.'

There was silence and he noticed that she was looking down at her food, rather than eating it.

'Is the meal okay?' he asked.

'It's incredible,' she said. 'The right amount of spice, and I love the bomli. I've never heard of it before.'

'It's a lizard fish. I think in the UK it's rather confusingly called Bombay duck, but I have absolutely no idea why.'

'Whatever the reason, it's lovely. It's all delicious.'

The stilted conversation ceased and silence stretched, and for the first time since Logan had met Chloe it threatened to be awkward. Eventually she looked up from her plate and smiled, but it was a smile that looked manufactured and it didn't reach her eyes.

'I was wondering if you or Belle had any favourite music. I suppose we should be thinking about what to have at the wedding, and then there are flowers to talk about or...'

'Or we could talk about what's bothering you,' he said, because he couldn't sit here knowing something was wrong. Not when he could see strain in her hazel eyes.

'Nothing's bothering me.'

'I thought you never lied,' he said softly, the words without sting. Her gaze flew to his before she set down her knife and looked away, and he followed her gaze, absorbing the deep green of the leafy trees, the glimpse of the sea that could be seen in the distance.

Then she took a deep breath and turned back to Logan. 'This morning, did I do something wrong? Or say something to upset you?'

'No. Absolutely not.' Logan felt a sharp pang of regret at his own behaviour. He'd hoped he'd carried it off, hoped that he hadn't shown the intensity of his frustration, the ire at himself that had made him wish he could kick himself round the block. But of course he had, and it had been a forlorn naivety to kid himself otherwise.

'You don't have to say that.' Her voice was clear and even. 'If you're worried about hurting my feelings, you don't need to. I won't back out of the wedding, or pull the rug from under your feet. I'd rather know if something is wrong or if you're having second thoughts about our agreement this morning. I'm not good at reading signs, so you need to tell me.'

Logan reached out. *Damn it.* He should

have known she'd feel like this; she'd told him about Mike and not being able to navigate a relationship.

'Chloe, I promise you did nothing wrong. I messed up, not you. This morning was nothing to do with you.' Or at least, not in a way that was her fault. *Jeez.* In a few scant days he had managed to both lose control, focus and hurt Chloe's feelings. The knowledge emphasised the need to pull back but first, and most importantly, he needed to make good the hurt.

She studied his expression. 'But something happened?'

Logan hesitated, knowing he owed Chloe an explanation, and wondered at her ready assumption that it was she who had done something wrong, when he had been the jackass. He owed her the truth.

'Yes. Something happened. I missed a call from my dad. He's been off-grid for months and he doesn't know about Belle's heart attack.'

'Oh.' Chloe raised a hand to her mouth. 'And you missed the call because of me.' Her voice was small and flat and it took a second for him to get it—Chloe thought this was her fault. She looked so stricken he instinctively reached out, covered her hand in his and imbued his voice with reassurance and truth.

'No. I missed the call because I didn't take my phone with me, because I forgot. That is on me, not you. One hundred percent on me.' The guilt was his to bear, not hers.

'And obviously he didn't reply when you called back.'

Logan shook his head. 'Didn't even go to voice mail. Not that it would have mattered if it had. I've left countless messages, texts, emails. But nothing back. Until this morning. He left a message saying he was off-grid, and he'd try again some time, and I haven't been able to get hold of him since. I've talked to tech wizards to see if they can trace where he is, figure out something.'

Anything. Because Belle deserved the chance to see her son, and Matt deserved the chance to come and make his peace in the event of the worst-case scenario. But now that wouldn't be possible, all because he'd given attraction, feelings, full rein.

'I'm sorry, Logan.'

He studied her face, sensing that the word was still half-apology, that Chloe still felt she was to blame.

'Thank you.' Before he could say any more, the waiter returned to clear their plates and hand them the dessert menu.

'You choose this time,' Chloe said as she rose to her feet. 'I'm just headed to the bathroom.'

'Sure.' Logan watched her walk away, determined to reassure her when she returned to the table, to try to erase the shadows in her eyes.

Chloe stood in the bathroom and stared at her reflection, willing her emotions to come under control. She would not make this about her, yet a sense of bleakness touched her. Once again, even if it had been unwittingly, she had brought harm. Because if Logan hadn't been involved with her he would never have forgotten about his phone. The idea, the confirmation, that she was a harbinger of doom twisted inside her and she pushed it down.

Dwelling on it wouldn't help. Perhaps what she should do was walk back to the table and bring their liaison to an end, but that would simply close the proverbial stable door after the horse had bolted. Instead she could try and help. Do something positive. Not just to ease her own sense of guilt, but because she knew, bone-deep, what it felt like to wish she could turn back the clock, alter a decision.

Determination flooded through her as she walked back to the table where the desserts waited and sat down.

'I ordered *puit d'amour*—a kind of pastry tart with coconut and vanilla filling—and a traditional flan that's a bit like a crème caramel. I thought we could share,' Logan explained.

'That sounds lovely.'

And it was, sweet, light and not too much. Logan waited until they had finished and then said, 'I want to say again—this is not on you.'

Chloe raised a hand. 'This isn't about me,' she said firmly. 'And in the end the blame game doesn't matter. What matters is what we do now.'

Logan raised an eyebrow. 'We?'

'Yes. I want to see if I can help locate your dad. I am sure that you have unearthed every stone, but sometimes fresh eyes can see something different.' She saw reservation on his face. 'Please let me try. It can't do any harm. I do so much research in my job, it may help.'

Logan hesitated and she sensed his reluctance, but sensed too that he was out of other options. 'Thank you. It's worth a shot. Where do we start?'

'When did you last see him?'

There was a short silence. 'Six years ago. In Mauritius.' Logan met her gaze, his eyes neutral. 'That's the last time I can be sure of his whereabouts, though I do know Belle received a postcard from Sydney nine months ago.' He gave a short laugh, devoid of mirth. 'We aren't a close family.'

Chloe realised how difficult this conversation must be; Logan was a private man. 'That's not true,' she said gently. 'You and Belle are close, that's obvious from everything you've said, everything you're doing for her. Including trying to find your dad, including answering my questions.'

'I appreciate what you're doing, that you want to help, but I have so little information about where my dad may be, that I am not sure you can.'

'Maybe I can't, but I'd still like to try, but only if you feel comfortable telling me everything you can think of about your dad that may trigger something. *Anything* at all.'

He studied her face for a long moment and

then gave a small nod and she knew whatever he was about to share meant something. She reached out, pushed their empty plates away and took his hand.

'My dad could be anywhere,' he began. 'He's travelled all my life, ever since I was born. Ever since my mother died.' His words impacted her with the tragic truth of them. 'Died giving birth to me.'

Chloe blinked back tears. 'I'm so, so sorry, Logan. That is awful, and devastating for you and your dad.'

'My dad has never got over it. And he has never forgiven me. Or Belle.'

Chloe frowned. 'But it wasn't your fault.'

'That's not how my father sees it. According to him, my mother and he didn't want a child. They wanted to travel together, be free spirits. He claims Belle emotionally blackmailed my mother into having a baby, so the Jamieson line could continue.'

Logan's face was grim now. 'According to Belle, my mum was thinking about starting a family and asked her opinion, which she gave, saying that from her perspective it would be nice to have a grandchild, someone to continue the line, but it was up to my mum and dad. There's no way now to know which version is true.'

'And you are in the middle.'

'In the end, it's Belle who has been there for me, but my dad believes my mother died to gratify my grandmother's ambition and I am the result. He can't forgive either of us for that.'

'There's nothing to forgive you for. You are completely innocent. You were a baby, you didn't choose to be born. You're his son, and you're also part of the woman he loved.'

'That's not how he sees it.' The words were said with starkness that she recognised and understood. 'He couldn't bond with me as a baby because every time he looked at me it brought back memories of what he'd lost. It still does. That's why he finds life easier if he doesn't see me.'

'Being a parent isn't about making your own life easier.' Chloe felt anger and sadness at the thought of a young Logan wondering why his father kept disappearing and wasn't there for him. And then, worse, to discover the reason why and to take on that guilt. 'He could have tried. He could have not run away.

He could have separated his grief at the tragedy from his love for his son.'

'Maybe he could have if I'd been a child he wanted.'

She looked at him, understanding the reality of the words. Maybe her mother could have forgiven Chloe if she'd been a child she'd wanted.

'As it is, I am the person who ruined his life.'

'He *should* have tried,' she repeated. 'And by not trying he lost out. He had a chance to have a relationship with you, watch you grow up into a good, successful man. Someone worth knowing. Because that's who you are.'

'Thank you.' His tone was neutral and she could only hope he believed her words. 'But none of what I've told you helps locate him.'

Chloe thought for a moment. 'Maybe, maybe not. It sounds as if he is nomadic, restless… Has he ever told you anything about a travel plan? Does he revisit places? What does he do when he is travelling? Does he tend to stay in five-star hotels or camp in the wilderness in a one-man tent?'

She stopped, seeing frustration and sadness on his face. 'I don't know. All I know is that he does seem to go to India quite a lot. I think that was where my parents were planning to start their travels. That's it. That's all I've got.'

'Maybe it will be enough. I'll do my best to see if I can come up with any ideas.' She took a last sip of coffee. 'Shall we head back?' she asked. She wanted to get started on trying to find Matt Jamieson. She wanted, needed, to do something.

He nodded as he rose to his feet. And as she looked at him, standing under the sweeping branches of the banyan tree, the lights glinting in his blond hair, she saw his strength but also the shadows in his eyes. Without thinking, she moved towards him and reached up to gently smooth the frown from his brow, wishing she could smooth the sadness away as easily.

'I'm sorry, Logan. Sorry you never had a chance to know your mother and I'm sorry she never had a chance to know you. She would have been proud of you.'

'I hope so,' he said, his voice gruff, and she heard the emotion there. And maybe so did he, because he took her hand in his, squeezed

168 THEIR MAURITIUS WEDDING RUSE

gently and then took a step back. 'Thank you,' he said. 'I wish it could have been more productive. But thank you for trying.'

His voice held a hint of finality, and she understood he wanted to bring the conversation to a close. And she understood why, as she too took a step back, knowing she had to match the physical action with an emotional one. She needed to create some space, and didn't want her own emotions to take over. She felt sadness at his loss, sadness and anger at how his father had treated him, but what threatened to overwhelm her was the intensity of her desire to offer comfort, to hold him, to protect him.

The idea was laughable. Logan didn't need or want her protection, or her comfort. Logan was a man who would see those emotions as a danger signal, and he would be right. Logan wanted what she had offered—practical help in finding his father. And that was what she would provide. She would start her search as soon as they got back to the villa.

CHAPTER TEN

LOGAN SHIFTED IN his sleep and opened his eyes, unsure of what had woken him, but aware of Chloe's presence by his side. He'd gone to bed first at Chloe's insistence, left her sat at the table in the living room, intent on following up an idea. Logan had wanted to stay but he hadn't, unsure if there was a hidden message in Chloe's insistence, that she wanted some space—that she would rather not share a bed, was moving away from the idea of intimacy.

If that was the case, Logan knew he should welcome it; he still felt shocked at the ease with which he'd confided in her. He could tell himself it had been done to aid the search for Matt, and that had been his motivation at the start, but the sense of being listened to—the depth of understanding in her hazel eyes, the sense she truly got it, a sense of closeness—had all combined and he'd shared more than he'd intended.

Which made him feel exposed, vulnerable almost, and so he welcomed the sense that she was pulling away—a reminder of his own earlier decision to do just that. Yet as he felt Chloe's warmth beside him now as she slept, her cheek pillowed on one hand, long eyelashes fringing her cheek, he felt a sudden pang. He got a sudden glimpse of why people did risk closeness, even as he knew it wasn't a risk he could take himself. That road was not for him; to take it would be inherently wrong. When he'd cost his parents so much. When he knew how much the loss of love could hurt.

He must have drifted back into sleep, because it was a little later when he opened his eyes again, this time sure that something wasn't right. Next to him, Chloe was mumbling, her movements restless, and then she gave a wrenching sob, followed by a cry as she half-sat up.

'No. Please. Please. No. Stop.' The sheer raw pain in her voice pierced him as he tried to work out what to do.

He touched her gently on her shoulder. 'Chloe. It's okay. It's Logan.'

At first she twisted away and then a minute later she opened her eyes which were flecked with pain, fear, panic and a desperation that twisted his heart.

'It's okay. I'm here. You're in Mauritius. You're safe. With me.' The words were instinctive.

Her breathing came in gulps as she clenched the duvet with her hands, still staring at him with unseeing eyes.

'It's me. Logan,' he repeated, and now her breathing slowed, her eyes dawning with recognition. She looked round the room, then back to him, clearly grounding herself. Pulled the duvet up closer, as though she was cold.

'I'm sorry,' she said. 'It was a dream. I'm fine now.'

But she didn't look fine. She looked exhausted, smudges of tiredness under eyes that still held remembered terror.

'I'll get up, have some water and do some work.'

He glanced at his watch and saw it was the early hours of the morning. 'I've got a better idea,' he said. 'We're going out for a walk,

172   THEIR MAURITIUS WEDDING RUSE

away from here. I'll bring breakfast, and we can watch the sun rise.'

Her face brightened a little. 'I'd like to get out,' she said. 'Get rid of the images in my head.'

'Then that's what we'll do.'

Half an hour later they were ready to go. Logan slung the rucksack containing breakfast onto his shoulder and held out his hand. Chloe still looked desperately vulnerable, her usual confidence, her sparkle, sapped by whatever horror the nightmare had contained. Now wasn't the time to worry about the sheer protective instinct he felt, or to quibble or analyse what hand-holding meant. He could only hope it offered some comfort.

They walked in silence, Logan hoping that the lush, tropical scenery would somehow bring some tranquillity to Chloe. They walked through magnificently regal palm groves, each tree topped with deep-green fronds that swayed gently in the early-morning breeze, bursts of colour provided by lotus flowers and an array of exotic flowers he couldn't name. Waxy-leaved, metre-high pineapple trees formed rosette shapes, whilst the much taller mango trees exuded a sweet smell from the clusters of white flowers that adorned them, contrasting with the bright-reddish purple of their large leaves. The whole thing created an avenue of beauty as they approached the small fishing village that was their destination.

'Now we're going to swap vegetation for the beach,' Logan said. 'A different type of beauty. We should be just in time for the sunrise.'

Ten minutes later they sat on the mostly deserted beach, with its nearly white sand. Chloe hugged her knees as she looked out over the spread of blue water, and she gave a small gasp as the very first rays of the sun peeped over the horizon in a tantalising glimpse of colour. It was as though a paint brush had taken to the sky, creating a breath-taking spectrum of orange, yellow and red that refracted over the blue of the waves lapping the shore. They sat and watched, seeing the fishermen haul their boats to shore and the nets of colourful freshly caught fish.

'Thank you for bringing me here,' she said softly.

'You're welcome. I hoped seeing the start of a new day may help counteract the night.'

'It has. I feel better, more at peace. Thank

174 THEIR MAURITIUS WEDDING RUSE

you.' She accepted the breakfast roll Logan offered her, a simple bread roll with cheese.

They ate in silence for a while and Logan wondered if he should say any more, but knew that perhaps he should leave it. But if he could help in any way, damn it he wanted to.

'Do you have nightmares often?' he asked gently.

'Less frequently now than I used to, but yes, they are recurring,' she said. 'But it's unlikely I'll have another so soon after last night's. You should be safe from a repeat performance. I am sorry you had to see it.'

'There's no need to apologise.' Why did she take so much blame for things that weren't her fault? 'If it does happen again, I'd rather be there to see if I can help.'

He studied her face and his heart gave a sudden twist in his chest at her sheer beauty. The magic hour of sunrise had tinged the air with a rose-pink glow that surrounded her in a magical ambiance, and seemed to showcase the lustre of her strawberry-blonde hair and accentuate the classic planes of her face, the slant of cheek bone, the line of her nose.

'There's nothing you can do,' she said.

'It may help to talk,' he said. 'This time—

here in Mauritius, you and me—it's our time. It's a bubble, and whatever we say here is confidential. It helped me to talk to you yesterday. Let me return the favour.'

She considered the words and then she nodded and began to speak. 'I told you my father and brother died in a car accident. What I didn't tell you is what happened. I was fifteen years old.'

She was looking at him, but Logan knew she was seeing something else, looking into the past. 'I was going through a rebellious phase. I took up with an unsavoury boyfriend, and that night I'd asked to go to a party and my parents said no. I pretended to agree, then sneaked out and went anyway. But it all went wrong. My boyfriend turned nasty and I got scared. I called my dad. He and my brother came to get me. They never made it. A lorry overturned them.'

Her voice cracked. 'All because of me. I've imagined it so many times, and that's what I dream about—the two of them next to each other, chatting, and then suddenly from nowhere the loom of the lorry, the fear, the panic…and then perhaps pain and fear. I don't know who died first, or if they were in agony. If they spoke to each other, if...'

'Jeez. I am so sorry.' He saw the terrible weight of guilt etched on her face, in the sag of her shoulders, and shifted across the sand to be next to her. As he pulled her against him, he wished he knew what to say, and finally decided on, 'It was a tragedy, but it wasn't your fault.'

'But it was,' Chloe said. 'If I hadn't lied, if I hadn't gone to that party, they would still be alive. It's that simple. It is on me.'

The raw conviction, the pain, in her voice seared his heart. 'Every single day hundreds, thousands, of teenagers do what you did. There was no possible way you could have predicted what would happen. And who knows? They may have decided to go out that night anyway. There are so many "what ifs" and maybes.'

'And one certainty. They were on that road coming to get me because I messed up.'

'It was an accident, a tragic, awful, terrible accident. You can't take responsibility for that. You can wish that it hadn't happened, but that's different from taking the blame, the responsibility. Isn't that what you would tell anyone else in your position?' He thought for a minute. 'What about your mother? Have you spoken to her about how you feel?'

'My mother will never forgive me,' she said flatly. 'And I don't blame her. She lost her husband, the love of her life, and her golden child, the son who she adored.'

'But she still had you.'

'She didn't want me. It's no secret that she wished it had been me instead of James. She said it herself.'

Anger touched him now, a cold burn that any parent, however grief-stricken, could say that to their child's face. 'This is not your fault, Chloe. And what about your loss?' he asked. 'You lost your father, your brother.'

There was a pause as she looked at him wide-eyed, almost as if this aspect hadn't occurred to her and he saw the tears in her eyes.

'I loved them. But my mother lost them through no fault of her own. Her grief takes priority.'

'No, it doesn't.' Logan took a deep breath and tried to tamp down the gamut of emotions running through him. 'I am not trying to belittle your mum's grief, but you are entitled to grieve as well, and your grief has been compounded by guilt you should have never been burdened with.'

'Yes. But that's just words.' Her voice echoed the words he himself had used the previous day and held despair, a sad knowledge. And he understood, he truly did. 'I know I am to blame. I know my mother is right.'

'No.' He shook his head. 'She isn't.' And in that moment his heart went out to her. That she had borne this burden for so long on her own... Logan had had Belle all his life but Chloe had had no one, just a mother who had heaped further coals on the flames of guilt and kept the fire burning. 'You are her child, the daughter she bore and looked after. So she should have been there for you. And, by blaming you, she has lost out on a chance to have a good relationship with you.'

She stared at him wide-eyed. 'That's pretty much what I said to you.'

'Yes, and the same goes for you. If you could only see it.' He pulled her close again so that her hair was tickling his cheek.

'But it's not that easy, is it?' she asked. 'To see it.'

'No,' he agreed. 'It isn't.'

They sat for a while and then he said, 'Tell

me about them. About your dad and about James. Maybe remembering them would help.'

Chloe turned to look at him. 'I'd like that.' She began to speak quietly. 'I adored my dad. He was a big bear of a man. He'd throw me in the air, push me high on the swings, take me on long walks. He also used to write poetry and we'd talk about the future, books, politics...

'James was six years older than me, a real big brother. He'd play with me; he taught me how to tie my shoelaces and taught me self-defence.' Her voice broke. 'I miss them,' she said.

'Of course you do, how could you not? But you were lucky to have them. They both sound like wonderful, loving family.'

'I'm sorry you didn't have that,' she said softly.

'I had Belle,' he said simply. 'She was truly remarkable, the way she managed to bring me up *and* make Belle's a global success. She'd take me to work with her, and I loved it. I got to know the staff, the products, the whole lot. I'd look forward to school holidays just so I could go to the office.'

He sensed Chloe tense slightly next to him,
and she looked at him with a slight question
in her eyes. 'So would you consider...?' she
began, and broke off.

'Consider what?' he asked.

CHAPTER ELEVEN

CHLOE SHIFTED A little away from the warm, reassuring bulk of Logan's body, wondering if she should say what she wanted to say, wondering whether it was any of her business. But they had just shared so much and…his description of his life with Belle had triggered a question. It had made her wonder and it felt important to follow it through, for Belle and for Logan.

'Would you consider succeeding Belle?' she asked simply. 'You know I had a meeting with Belle before we came to Mauritius. Belle asked me to give her options, the best way forward for the company. She's concerned that she is the face of the company and without her the company will suffer.'

Logan nodded. 'I know.'

'I advised her that the best thing she could do is choose a successor, or a team of successors. Get them into the public eye. Create reassurance.'

'Did she agree?'

'Yes. But she was adamant it couldn't be a family member. That didn't make sense then and it doesn't make sense now. Surely she would like you to take over?'

'I know that's what she wants.' His voice was low. 'But I can't give her that.'

'Because it's not what you want?' Chloe asked.

'I *can't* work for Belle's, can't succeed her.'

'Why not?' she asked, though she suspected the answer.

'Because then…my mother would have died so the line could continue, sacrificed on the altar of Belle's ambition. I owe her memory more than that. I owe my father more than that. I know how much it would hurt him if I got involved with the company. In fact, he once forbade me to do it.'

'Even if it would make you happy?'

'That doesn't matter, when I've already cost him his happiness.'

'So if you had free choice you'd have got involved with Belle's?'

'In a heartbeat. I hate not being able to do something that is so important to her.'

Chloe shook her head. 'I meant what do *you* want to do, Logan? Not for Belle or for your dad. For your own happiness.'

There was silence and she raised a hand to push back an errant strand of hair. 'I know that's a massive, complicated question.' She looked around at the pristine white sand bordered by the turquoise blue waves, warmed by the early morning sun, but warmed too by Logan's kindness, his compassion. She wanted to try to help Logan be happy. 'Whatever you decide, don't do what I did,' she said.

'What do you mean?'

'You asked me once, why corporate law, and I didn't tell you the truth. Or not the full truth.'

'You said you want to be the best.'

'And that was true. But I don't want it for me. Being a corporate lawyer wasn't my dream. It was my brother's. It's what James was planning to do. It was his holy grail.'

'And you took on his dream.'

She nodded. 'It seemed like the only way to get my mother to look on me with even a hint of liking. It allows a bit of him to live on for her, keeps his memory alive.'

'But what about you, stuck in a pressurised job, a career that you didn't choose?'

She shook her head. 'I did choose it, and I don't regret that choice. It is the right thing to do, the only way I have to try to make up to my mother for a little of what she lost. I am doing what I have to do. Your choice isn't constrained by guilt. Your father chooses to place blame where there is none and that is affecting the decisions you are making. You don't owe him your happiness. If taking a position at Belle's would make you happy, you should do it. That's what I think.' She pressed her lips together. 'But I know it's not that easy, and I promise I won't say any more about it.'

'And I promise to think about what you've said, if you promise to think about what I am about to say.'

'Sure.' And she'd keep the promise, even though she knew nothing he could say could alter the course she'd chosen.

'I admire what you've done, and I understand why you've done it.' His hand, holding hers, was warm, assured, making her feel safe, cared for, listened to. 'But it doesn't seem right that you should sacrifice your dreams. I just wonder if there is another way for you to try to forge a relationship with your mother. This is your life. You only get one shot. I want you to live it, to enjoy it, to follow your own dream.'

'I...' Chloe looked into his eyes, saw sincerity, belief and warmth, and a sense of panic set in. What was her dream? Just now, she no longer knew, but she knew that the setting, the place, the pull and tug of attraction, the kisses and the connection were messing with her head. Making her believe the impossible, making her think the illusion could be reality, and it couldn't.

'That's what I want for you too,' she said softly.

She smiled at him and felt her heart turn in her chest, as again illusion sought to take over, and she forced herself to turn away. Felt a palpable sense of relief when her phone pinged a notification.

'It's the bridal shop. My dress has come in.'

The final costume for the ultimate finale of the illusion. An apt reminder, perhaps, of what they were really here to do; a natural time to step away from the confidences they had shared. Because, whilst Chloe didn't regret these past hours, she had to get her head together and keep perspective. Remember what was real and what was not. Remember that their relationship had an end date baked in.

'There's a lot more as well. We need to sort out flowers, buy the rings... What about your wedding outfit?'

'I asked Celeste to sort out my clothes—I thought there was a small chance someone may recognise my name and it may ignite publicity.'

'Good call. I didn't mention you at all in the bridal shop.' Chloe thought of the dress she'd chosen and felt a pinprick of doubt. It was nice enough. It would do the job. That was all that mattered.

A mantra she repeated to herself as they walked back through the picturesque fishing village, admiring the brightly coloured houses and craft shops along the way.

They continued to sightsee during the car journey to the town.

'I'll go and get the dress,' she said, and he nodded.

'Leave the flowers to me and I'll meet you

back here. We can head back to the market for more *dholl puris* and pineapples.'

'Sounds good.'

Too good, she thought as she made her way to the bridal shop, trying to process how different everything seemed since she had first come and picked her dress just the day before. Then she'd been confused, worried she'd done something to upset Logan and worried she couldn't read the signs right. Now she'd shared things she'd never dreamt she'd share and suddenly she wondered if she'd made a mistake. Would it be possible to treat this time as a bubble, to return to a professional status quo, forget all they'd said, forget how they'd held each other and forget the kisses and the confidences?

She entered the shop and told herself that of course it was possible. Because anything else was unthinkable.

'Hi, Anne. I've come to pick up my dress.'

'Great. I'll get it for you. But…' The young woman hesitated, then continued, 'We've had some new stock come in. I wondered if you wanted to have a quick look.'

Chloe thought of the dress she'd chosen. There was nothing wrong with it, but it hadn't made her heart sing. Which was fine, but curiosity got the better of her. 'There's no harm in having a quick look.'

The assistant beamed. 'No harm at all. After all, this is your day, and you want to wow your fiancé—make sure you are a vision he will never forget.'

Chloe paused as the words hit home and she realised she did want to wow Logan—did want to stun him and knock him for six. She wanted to be etched on his memory. After all, just because this was a fake wedding didn't mean it couldn't be special or memorable. So why not give him one glorious knock-out bridal vision?

'Bring it on,' she said.

The assistant turned and went to the back room, returning with a dress that had Chloe rooted to the spot. Even draped in Anne's arms it was beautiful, the embroidered organza material falling in a glorious flow.

'It's gorgeous, isn't it?' Anne said and Chloe could only nod.

'Would you like to try it on?'

Another nod and fifteen minutes later she surveyed her reflection. It was as if the dress had been made for her. It was elegant, svelte, feminine and unquestionably bridal. The A-line style flattered her figure, emphasising her slender waist, and left her shoulders bare.

An image of Logan bending down and running kisses over her bare skin brought a flush to her face and heat to her body. The material fell from her waist to the floor in graceful folds, fanning out into a small train. The whole dress was covered in three-dimensional dahlia and daisy appliqué that made it both beautiful and unique.

It was stunning and, damn it, did make her heart sing. As she looked at her reflection now, it was as if she could see a Chloe from an alternate universe, a Chloe whose family had remained intact. That Chloe had her father by her side to give her away on her wedding day, James as an usher and his children the bridesmaid and ring-bearer. Her mother had helped her choose a dress, put together a guest list and arrange a seating plan.

It was a universe in which Lisa hadn't died, in which Logan had a mother and father and in which he was heir to Belle's with everyone's blessing.

But that universe wasn't real. Couldn't be real. But perhaps for one day she could be that Chloe—the Chloe who wore a dress that made her heart sing, a dress that would poleaxe Logan. Perhaps the wedding day could be made memorable for them both because they could never have the real thing. So she'd make it the best most magical illusion she could.

'I'll take it,' she said.

CHAPTER TWELVE

Two days later

LOGAN OPENED HIS EYES, aware that today was important: his wedding day. Correction, his fake wedding day. The idea was strangely sobering; the idea of standing with Chloe, making vows they both knew to be false, set his nerves on an unexpected edge.

Perhaps because he fully understood now what an enormous thing that would be for Chloe, to lie in front of witnesses, when she believed it was her lies that had caused her father's and brother's deaths, ended their lives and ruined her mother's. Yet she'd agreed, motivated by a desire to help Belle, and for that Logan was truly grateful. So today might not be real, simply the culmination of an illusion, but he wanted to use the day to show Chloe how grateful he was to her and wanted to make it as special as it was possible for it to be.

He hoped she had at least been heartened by Belle's demeanour the previous day. Despite the long journey, his grandmother had seemed stronger, clearly thrilled to be back in Mauritius and to see Celeste and Marie. Logan had stayed in Belle's villa whilst Chloe had gone back to their villa, everyone insistent that the groom shouldn't see the bride the evening before the big day.

Because they all believed Logan and Chloe had a lifetime together, rather than the few days they'd actually have. There'd be the wedding day today, then he and Chloe planned to spend the next few days with Belle, before the return to London and the operation. And then...then he and Chloe would be over.

The thought brought a bleakness he refused to acknowledge. Maybe he would miss Chloe, but that fact in itself made it imperative he got off the roller-coaster soon before it became an ever riskier, ever more dangerous ride of plummeting highs and lows. That was not for him.

Logan got up, knowing he now needed to focus on the preparations for the day.

Twenty minutes later, he entered the kitchen to find Marie preparing Belle's breakfast.

'How are you feeling?' she asked.

Logan thought for a minute. 'Nervous,' he said, and realised it was the truth. He didn't want to mess things up at this juncture, but he also didn't want this day to be any more difficult than it would be for Chloe. 'Has Celeste gone to Chloe?'

'Yes, she has. And trust me she knows what she's doing. She got me ready for my wedding, and her three granddaughters ready for theirs. Chloe is in good hands. So you just focus on getting everything done here. Let's make it a perfect day.'

'That sounds like a plan.'

In fact, why settle for just making the day 'as special as possible'? Why not go out and see if he could actually make it *special*, fullstop? A day Chloe would remember for the rest of her life, and look back on with a smile on her face, because it had been a day when she'd felt appreciated? Appreciation that it seemed no one had granted her since the tragedy—definitely not her mother and it sounded to him as though Mike had failed her too. Chloe had described supporting his football team, cooking his favourite foods... which sounded to Logan to have been a one-sided appreciation society. Today would be different.

Three hours later, Logan surveyed his reflection and ran through the list of preparations and the itinerary.

The villa was perfectly located, set on sun-warmed golden sands. A wooden walkway led down to a small enclosure that overlooked the sea, a spreading vista of azure that glinted and refracted in the sunlight. Logan had strewn the planks with flower petals, and the enclosure itself was draped with a concoction of exotic, sweet-smelling flowers woven together in flowing bursts of colour, interlaced with tendrils of leafy greenery, everything sending out an evocative, exotic perfume. A perfect romantic backdrop for the ceremony.

He thrust his hand into his pocket, checked that the wedding ring was there and ran through in his head the music he'd chosen. He'd wanted a live performer, but had been stumped by the problem of publicity. A problem circumvented by a stroke of luck: the celebrant's wife was an accomplished singer and had agreed to sing before the ceremony.

Another check of his reflection and he saw an image there he'd never thought to see:

Logan Jamieson, groom. *Temporary groom*, he reminded himself. Yet, having immersed himself in getting ready, in thoughts of Chloe, somehow it had become hard to remember that.

Which presumably explained the clutch of nerves in his gut, the sense of anticipation and a burning desire to see Chloe. He was on edge and exhilarated, filled with adrenalin. And, however much he told himself it was just nerves about whether they could pull this off, it felt like more than that. Another swoop on the roller-coaster. Too many emotions. But for today, for the days that were left, he was going to go with it. He would deal with the fallout at the end.

He reached up, adjusted his cravat, the pattern threaded with a colour that matched the flecks of green in Chloe's eyes. The grey suit was a mix of the traditional and contemporary, and his socks had a pineapple motif, chosen to make her smile.

He turned away from his image and made his way downstairs where the celebrant and his wife had arrived. He greeted them and then walked towards the flower-strewn enclosure where the ceremony would take place

196 THEIR MAURITIUS WEDDING RUSE

and where Belle was seated. Felt a surge of protective love for his grandmother, an admiration for her spirit and determination.

'You look beautiful,' he said, and she did—elegant and svelte in a pink suit, her hair styled in a soft, layered cut, a genuine smile on her face and some colour in her cheeks. A far cry from the woman of a week before who had sounded so distressed at the thought of leaving Logan alone.

This was the right thing to do.

'I am happy,' she said simply. 'To be here. And that you have found happiness.' Belle took his hand in hers. 'If you hadn't told me about Chloe, I would never have been motivated to come back here to Mauritius, wouldn't have spent the past days with a purpose. No matter what happens, I am grateful for that.'

For an instant Logan wondered if his grandmother had an inkling that all of this was an illusion for her benefit. But, looking down into her bright-blue eyes that met his straight on, he told himself he was being silly. Belle must be talking about the possibility of the operation going wrong. But now, seeing this rejuvenated, revitalised Belle, he could hope and believe that nothing would go wrong.

'No matter what, you are going to be alright,' he said, and she squeezed his hand.

'Not even you can control fate, Logan,' she said. 'But I think you're right. But, no matter what, always know I feel blessed to have you in my life. Now go and marry Chloe.'

Logan turned away from Belle as Marie and Celeste came to stand on either side of her, followed by the celebrant, who stood off to one side. Logan was aware of the beat of his heart pounding his rib cage, of a rush of feelings.

And then he saw Chloe walking towards him and everything else faded so that all he could see was her, radiant, heart-stopping and beautiful, a fairy-tale vision. He felt something wrench inside him, but immediately shut it down, reminding himself that neither he nor Chloe had any interest in real love or commitment. But that didn't mean that this wasn't important, because it was. This incredible woman had taken this on in order to help, to do good, and now she was walking alone down the flower-strewn walkway towards him, playing her part without support. And that felt wrong.

THEIR MAURITIUS WEDDING RUSE

* * *

Chloe saw the flowers strewn over the wooden boards, listened to the strains of the music as she took each step and heard the words of the song drift across the sun-laden air mingling with the hum of insects and the salty tang of the sea. It was the same song she and Logan had danced to a few nights before, the dance that had preluded a starlit kiss, and a night she knew she would never forget.

She looked across at him, saw the expression on his face as he took in her appearance and something caught in her chest, an undefinable tug of so many emotions—joy that she'd elicited this response in him, the shellshocked gaze of a man transfixed, alongside a bittersweet sensation of illusion blurring with reality and a wish for might have been. And then she saw him break with tradition and start to walk towards her, and her face lit up with an instinctive smile.

He reached her and took her hands in his and it felt as though it were just the two of them.

'You look magical,' he said. 'More beautiful than any man deserves.'

She smiled up at him. 'Is that what you

came to tell me?' she asked, a sudden sense of lightness uplifting her.

'Partly. But I also wanted to thank you, to say I understand the enormity of what I asked you to do. We are in this together and I wanted to walk with you, beside you.'

And now warmth touched her and she took his hand in hers as they turned to see Belle smiling at them. She saw Celeste wipe a surreptitious tear from her eyes, saw Marie give a nod of approval, and then together they walked towards the celebrant. The strains of music still surrounded them; the singer's voice singing words of love came to an end as they arrived at the wooden enclosure. Chloe looked out at the stretching vista of the sunlit sea, the cresting birds swooping towards the waves and the distant line of the horizon.

'Shall we begin?' the celebrant asked, and she nodded. They followed his instructions and, as they made the vows that Chloe knew were a lie, she felt the strength of Logan's fingers around hers and knew he was reminding her of why they were doing this. And, when she remembered all she had learnt about his past, she felt at peace.

Then Logan dug into his pocket and pulled

out a box containing the wedding ring he'd chosen for her, a stunning rose-gold band with mix of yellow gold swirled in, a gentle curve to it. And then Celeste handed her the box containing the one she had chosen for Logan, a gold band with a wood inlay. As she slipped it onto his finger there was a zinging sense of connection, as if some sort of promise had been made.

'I now pronounce you man and wife. You may kiss the bride.'

Chloe tipped her face up and as Logan's lips touched hers she felt a heat so intense, she thought she may burst into flame, her whole being subsumed in a sense of wonder. Saw from the intent look on his face—almost of shock—that he felt the same.

Whoa. This wasn't how it was supposed to be. The illusion was not meant to have this depth, this substance. Yet there was nothing she could do about it, nothing except try and deploy the voice of reason, the reminder that this was temporary, would be over in a few days and that soon she and Logan would be professional associates. The rings would be taken off and put away, the vows dissipated and lost in the world of professional reality.

And she would be good with that, once she was back in the real world—the world of work and lawsuits, of clients and the pursuit of ambition—this would all become insubstantial, dream-like. Wouldn't it? Doubts crystallised as she stood back, looked up into his face and saw the strength of the planes and angles, the warmth in his eyes; as she recalled the past days, the magic of his touch, the way he'd held her, listened to her and made her feel worthwhile.

All that would be gone. Bleakness touched her and she saw concern in his face at her small shiver.

'Are you okay?' he murmured.

'Yes. I'm fine.' Chloe tilted out her chin, clenched her hands into fists and then relaxed. Perhaps she would miss this a bit but, after all, she had only known Logan for a week, and there was no way he could have got into her heart or head enough to overthrow years of work and ambition. She would be fine, and if not she'd deal with that later. She refused to let bleak thoughts take away from today, from the time they did have.

So she smiled up at him and stood on tiptoe to brush his lips with her own once more before they turned to embrace Belle. They saw the happiness in the older woman's face, then hugged Celeste and Marie in turn, before thanking the celebrant and his wife.

'Now for some food,' Celeste said.

'And cake.'

The next hour was spent eating and talking, and Chloe felt a warm sense of satisfaction as she saw Logan sitting next to his grandmother and saw Belle's evident happiness.

'And now,' Belle said, beaming, 'I have a surprise for you. A car is arriving to take you to a five-star luxury resort for a three-day honeymoon.'

Logan and Chloe exchanged glances. She wasn't sure what she read in his brown eyes, even as she started to say, 'But we were going to—'

'Spend time with me? Nonsense. You deserve a honeymoon, not sitting around chatting to me.'

A three-day honeymoon. The thought made Chloe's head whirl; three days and nights with Logan. Just Logan and her, with no wedding to plan, in five-star luxury. An alarm bell clanged a danger signal and told her spending more time with him in a dream setting, without anyone else around, would mess with her head.

Worse, it may mess with her heart. Yet somehow, though she knew she should intervene to stop this idea, she didn't want to. Instead she wanted to throw caution to the wind for three days with Logan; to revel in his touch, his closeness; to hold and be held, talk and be listened to, to be herself.

No...to be the Chloe she maybe could have been if her path had been a different one. The temptation was too much to resist, even if she knew there might be hurt ahead. It was a price she would pay because she knew with complete certainty that, whatever she wanted, head or heart, in three days it would be over. Had to be over, because this time here could not be translated to a permanent reality.

It was not real. Could never be real. Because love and commitment were an impossibility for her. She would never risk hurting Logan, bringing doom or pain to him, and would never again raise her mother's hopes of a family.

But that didn't mean she couldn't have a three-day honeymoon. If that was what Logan wanted too.

Belle looked determined. 'I want you to go. I will be well looked after here; I'll spend time catching up with friends.' Something in her voice pulled Chloe from her own thoughts and she studied the older woman's face and saw a twinkle in Belle's bright-blue eyes.

Logan had obviously seen the same, and his eyes narrowed in suspicion. 'What friends?' he asked and Belle's eyes sparkled now.

'Bertrand got in touch. He read about my heart attack and contacted Celeste, and he's asked to see me. And I have agreed.'

Logan frowned. 'But the doctors said...'

'No stress or agitation. Bertrand knows that.'

'I should meet him,' Logan said doggedly.

'Nonsense. I have had a heart attack. I am not in my dotage. If there are any signs of trouble, I will ask him to leave. Besides, I will have Celeste and Marie here to guard my interests. This is not negotiable, Logan. I am seeing Bertrand, and you and Chloe are having a honeymoon. This is important to me. I promise to give you regular updates on my health.'

'And so will we,' Marie chipped in. 'We will look after her. You two go.'

* * *

An hour later, they were *en route*, waved off in a shower of confetti and flowers. Logan turned to Chloe. 'Are you alright with the honeymoon idea?' he asked.

'Yes, as long as you're okay leaving Belle?'

'I think if we hadn't left she would have had us kidnapped and forcibly taken to the resort.'

'She did seem very determined,' Chloe said. 'And that's a good sign, isn't it? The fact she is so…strong. But if you feel we should stay closer to the villa or stay with Belle, we should turn back.'

Logan considered her words. In truth, he felt optimistic about Belle's health and about the operation. He had been able to accept her insistence they go on a honeymoon without a qualm on that score.

His qualms were of a different nature. His emotions felt topsy turvy, still seesawing from watching Chloe walk towards him in the fairy-tale dress. Now here they were on their honeymoon. A honeymoon that wasn't real, another knock-on effect of their original deception. A normal, honeymoon couple would be full of hope for their future, would be making plans for the rest of their lives. He and Chloe only had a few days and that thought imbued him with…a sense of sadness.

He had to get a grip. This was just a reaction to having a relationship with the finish line already set. Until now, any relationship had simply fizzled out. Just like this one surely would have, given time. But, however this liaison would end, it *had* to end. That was a given. He could never offer love; he wouldn't risk what that emotion did to you. Loving someone was too high a risk. It took control, changed a person, and could bring grief, hurt and pain to oneself and others, innocent people caught in the crossfire. They both knew that. And he knew love was not for him, not when his birth had inadvertently destroyed it.

So he had a choice. He could brood over what he couldn't have, and didn't even want to have, or he could enjoy the next three days… and, more importantly, make sure that Chloe did too. She hadn't had a holiday in years and, once she was back home, who knew when she would again?

'I think it's okay to leave her. It's what she wants, and we can go back if there is even a hint of a problem. I trust Celeste or Marie to call me. If you're happy to keep driving to the resort, so am I.'

There was the heartbeat of a pause, as if she was reviewing something in her mind, and then she gave a small, decisive nod. 'I'm happy to keep driving,' she said, and he felt his own lips upturn into an answering grin.

CHAPTER THIRTEEN

HALF AN HOUR later they arrived, climbed out of the car and looked around at the idyllic scenery of the resort, a massive stretch of lush tropical greenery and lawns leading to a wide, curving bay of sand and the blue of the sea, dark now in the fragrant, dusky air. The whole thing spoke a promise of peace and tranquillity. A smiling staff member arrived, introduced herself as Tori, took their details and led them to their villa.

'It's gorgeous,' Chloe breathed, and it really was. The thatched building with stone-washed walls was set in its own private garden complete with private pool, terraced area, gazebo and stunning ocean views. The inside was exquisite, the high-ceilinged rooms and natural colours giving a sense of space and luxury. The bedroom had a four-poster bed that looked to combine comfort and opulence, the living area had an over-sized sofa and arm chairs and a glass coffee table.

The bathroom with its massive sunken tub and spacious walk in-shower elicited a 'Wow!' from Chloe.

'We hope you enjoy your stay,' Tori said. 'There are plenty of activities you can book or you can spend the day lying on the beach or by the pool. It is entirely up to you. Please let me know if you want to book into one of our restaurants. Or, if you prefer, you could order room service and eat whilst you watch the sunset from your terrace.'

Chloe glanced at Logan. 'We will probably order room service a bit later,' she said, and he agreed. That way he'd have Chloe all to himself. On a practical level, there was also no chance of being spotted.

'Just order via the tablet on the table and enjoy.'

With a smile, Tori left and, absurd though it was, Logan felt almost shy. The idea brought a smile to his face and Chloe looked at him questioningly.

'What's so funny?'

'I'm not sure. I feel…'

'Odd?' she suggested. 'I know what you

mean. We didn't expect this time—time for just us. The last week we've been caught up in the wedding, in Belle...and I know how worried you must have been, must still be. I know now how much she means to you and why. But now, here we are without a wedding to plan. Belle is in safe hands and there is just us.'

Just them. Just Logan and Chloe.

'But... I've been thinking, and we should use this time...time together...with a spark, liking, respect and fun.' She smiled at him 'I think you deserve that. Belle has done us proud with this place, but you have done her proud. You really have, Logan. Your idea, it has given her inner peace and strength. That, combined with her strength of mind, her spirit and her will to live will help her to prevail. You've done everything you can so that she is best placed to make it. That means something.'

He stepped towards her and tipped up her face. 'I couldn't have done it without you.' The words were no more than truth.

'I'm glad you didn't,' she said.

He smiled down at her and bent his head to brush his lips against hers. And now the atmosphere changed and sweetness seemed to morph into something else as desire tugged deep in his gut and pooled in her hazel eyes as she deepened the kiss before standing back.

'That four-poster bed looked pretty inviting,' she said. 'Why don't we work up an appetite for dinner?'

His desire deepened, pulsated, and he laughed as exhilaration and anticipation combined. He took her by the hand and they half-walked, half-ran towards the bedroom.

Logan opened his eyes feeling full of energy, buoyant and…happy. Somehow he and Chloe had tumbled into bed at dusk the previous evening and remained there. A quick check of the time showed him that it was already late morning.

For an instant the movement of the hands on his watch tinged his happiness with a sense of urgency, a realisation that the clock was ticking down. That soon the honeymoon period would be over and so would his time with Chloe; the boundaries would be redrawn. For a second, one tick of time, his whole being rebelled against the thought. Why ration happiness like this? But he knew the answer: because happiness didn't last and, even if it did for other people, it certainly wasn't meant for him.

So, best to live in the moment. He climbed out of bed and went in search of Chloe, finding her sat curled up on the sofa with her laptop in front of her.

'Tell me you aren't working,' he said.

'I'm not. And I don't even feel guilty. I know how hard I'll be working when I get back. I won't have time for anything else.' The words were said with resolution and he wondered if she too was having to remind herself of incoming reality.

'So what are you doing?'

She paused, then looked up at him. 'I haven't forgotten or given up on the idea of finding your father. I had an idea and...'

She turned the screen towards him. He looked at a photograph on which Chloe had zoomed in. 'That's my dad,' he said. Matt Jamieson stood at a festival of flowers in India amongst other spectators, a garland around his neck, dressed in a brightly coloured shirt and shorts.

'It's a picture from a recent online article. It places him in India and his name is actually mentioned in the caption—his first name, not his surname—and I thought there might be a chance the reporter may know him. Or the organisers may. The caption says he's a regular attendee. It's a long shot but...'

'It's a starting point. You're a genius.' Warmth touched him that Chloe had persevered, despite everything else there had been to do and to think about. 'I'll get onto to it now.'

The idea that there was a chance of finding his dad before the operation buoyed him. 'Then I could do with breakfast.'

Half an hour later he returned as Chloe emerged from the bathroom, clad in a teal-blue swimsuit, strawberry-blonde hair cascading to her shoulders in silky, smooth waves. 'I ordered breakfast,' she said. 'A floating breakfast, which we eat in the private pool.'

After a quick shower he changed into swimming trunks, to find Chloe already in the pool. She grinned up at him.

'Look!' She gestured to the floating basket tray that held pastries, bread rolls, fruit and coffee, all interspersed with a variety of artfully placed brightly blooming fresh flowers, creating a tableau of food that somehow coasted safely on the flat blue water of the pool.

214 THEIR MAURITIUS WEDDING RUSE

Chloe was perched on the side and he sat next to her, the warmth of the sun warming their backs, and he watched as she carefully picked up the coffee, then sat back slightly.

'This is incredible,' she said, waving a hand towards the view, the mountains off to one side a jagged, undulating line, and then ahead of them in the distance lay the spread of azure water of the bay.

'I thought we could head out on a catamaran ride after breakfast,' he suggested.

'That sounds dreamy. That's what all this feels like,' she said softly. 'A dream.' There was wistfulness in her voice. 'One I want to enjoy while it lasts.'

One that they would have to wake up from, in the knowledge that it couldn't be repeated. The unspoken words seemed to hang in the sunlit air and he hurried into conversation.

'Talking of dreams, there's something I want to talk to you about.' Whilst he still could, before he was constrained by professional boundaries.

'Go ahead.'

'I know you're fulfilling your brother's dreams, and I understand why, but I just wanted to finish the conversation we had on the beach, where I said you should think about following your own dream…' He shrugged. 'You asked me what would make me happy, now I'm asking you the same.'

Her eyes widened, partly in surprise, partly in thought. 'I don't know,' she admitted.

'Then maybe here is a good place to think about it, whilst you are a long way from home, a long way from the office.' He wanted her to think about it, wanted her perhaps to realise she could live her own dream. 'Maybe if you work it out it could be something to aspire to later, once you have achieved partnership. I mean, what did you want to be when you were younger?'

Chloe steadied the tray, lifted it up, deposited it on the side of the pool, picked up a croissant and kicked her legs gently in the water, the ripples spreading. 'Maybe a teacher, or a social worker, or to work for a charity. I wanted to do something that made a difference to people's lives.' She shook her head. 'But that's over now.'

'It doesn't have to be. You still can do it, can still dream about it. It's okay to have your own dreams.' It seemed important to him that she knew that, that this vital, vibrant Chloe could have a dream of her own. 'Promise you'll think about it.'

'I promise. As long as you keep your promise to do the same—about Belle's.'

'Deal.'

She held out her hand and he put his into it. 'Deal,' she said and then, before he knew what she was going to do, she gave an impish grin. 'Enough serious stuff now,' she said, and with a deft tug she pulled them both into the water. 'Last one to the other side buys lunch,' she said and started swimming across the pool.

Without further ado he started after her and caught her as she surfaced, and she gave a gurgle of laughter as he grabbed her and pulled her against him. 'I win,' he said. 'And I have a much better forfeit.' He wiggled his eyebrows and she laughed again.

'Tell me,' she whispered.

So he did, and within minutes they were scrambling out of the pool, dripping wet, and heading back to the villa.

Much later they left the villa, walked down the terracotta pathway through the lush gardens, inhaling the fragrant scents of hibiscus and frangipani, walking through trees that shaded stone statues of elephants and past aqueduct features where falls of water flowed, the sound mingling with the coos and caws of exotic birds.

Hand in hand, they crossed a verdant lawn and headed towards the bay and the catamaran they'd booked. Chloe tried to remember the last time she'd felt this happy, this relaxed, this safe. Looking down at their linked hands, she remembered the feel of those hands on her body and against all odds felt a thrill of renewed desire, along with the sweet knowledge that they had another two nights, another two days. She refused to think beyond that, and was relieved when Logan's phone pinged and distracted her.

He pulled it out of his pocket, looked at it and smiled. 'It's from Belle. A picture of her and Bertrand.'

Halting, he handed the phone to Chloe and she studied the picture of a dapper elderly man with a head of thick silver hair, deep-brown eyes and a wide smile sitting next to a smiling Belle, who had captioned the picture 'better than medicine'.

'They look happy,' she said. 'It looks like it

218   THEIR MAURITIUS WEDDING RUSE

is a good thing they reconnected. Maybe it's given them a chance to make peace.'

'That would mean a lot to Belle. She never forgot Bertrand, I know that.'

The words made Chloe pause. Would Logan ever forget her? Of course not, but her memory would fade, he'd start a new relationship, then after a while another. And she— what would she do? Would she do the same? Embark on more liaisons hidden from her mother? The idea made her feel desolate, and suddenly the sun seemed a little less bright, the lush surroundings a little less verdant.

Chloe shook the feeling away as they approached the golden sands and the catamaran, determined not to let anything spoil this day, to allow no thoughts of the future to intrude. A few minutes later, they boarded, and a crew member explained the day would include snorkelling and a barbecue.

'And of course relaxing and enjoying the scenery. Together.'

Chloe smiled her thanks and then smiled at Logan as they set off, not caring if the smile held a hint of goofiness. Right here, right now, she felt aglow with happiness, sitting in a catamaran on water as smooth as glass, as blue as a sheet of turquoise and watching the shimmer and dart of shoals of fish through the glass bottom of the boat.

She was full of anticipation at the idea of the day ahead as they made their way to the front of the boat where there was an area covered in netting and complete with plumped-up cushions to relax on. Settled down with Logan's warm bulk next to her, she let herself get lost in the beauty of the surroundings, at the mountains in the distance, the expanse of blue and the sound and sights of the birds as they swooped and dived towards the waves.

They went in closer to the shore towards craggy rocks and mangroves, and the glory of a waterfall loomed up above them, the water cascading down, so close it felt possible to stand and shower.

As they headed back out again, she sat back with a smile at Logan, and he smiled as he put his arm round her waist and pulled her to him, opening his mouth to say something…

But the words were destined never to be spoken as the ring of her phone came from her bag, the ring tone a shock from the outside world. It was her mother. Why would her mother be calling her?

CHAPTER FOURTEEN

CHLOE SCRABBLED IN her bag, and pulled out the phone just as Logan's rang. She put the receiver to her ear as he did the same, the motions almost comical in their synchronicity. Almost.

'Mum, are you okay?'

'Is it true?' Janet's voice came down the line, the tone one of suppressed excitement.

'Is what true?' Chloe asked, a sense of trepidation unleashing in her tummy.

'Have you married Logan Jamieson?'

Chloe turned to look at Logan, who was looking as shell-shocked as she, the phone already disconnected. 'Tell them no comment,' he said.

'I'm really sorry, Mum. I'll have to call you back.'

She dropped the phone and stared at him wide-eyed, eyes now only for him.

'What's happened?'

'Somehow the press have got hold of the story. That was a reporter asking if it was true I'd got married.'

Chloe's brain scrambled as she stared out at the still-azure water, wondering how it could still look the same, with the fish still swimming, their brightly coloured bodies weaving through the water. She tried to work out the repercussions, the consequences, desperately trying to tell herself not to panic, not to dramatize. Told herself that somehow this could be contained, be controlled.

Her mother's voice rang in her ears with its hardly ever heard strain of excitement, of potential approval. Because her mum thought she was finally on the way to being a grandmother, that there was a chance of a baby. A boy. Another James. Now Chloe would have to tell her it wasn't true, wasn't happening, and she would dash her hopes and disappoint her all over again.

She'd have to confess that once again she'd lied. How could she have done this—agreed to a deception of this magnitude that could have such far-reaching consequences? It all showed she hadn't really changed from that foolish girl of sixteen. The knowledge twisted her insides.

Logan looked at his watch, then around to where the crew were glancing over at them.

'We'd better get back to the resort. Figure this out, what it means and what we can do to contain it.'

Damage control... Chloe grabbed the lifeline. There must be something they could do, some way to fend this off to make sure her mother didn't hope and dream, only to have those hopes bitterly disappointed yet again.

Logan turned off his phone. 'Better not to receive any more calls till we have a plan.'

Chloe nodded assent and did the same. The return trip seemed interminable, the scenery no longer worthy of notice, its beauty remote now, a sign that nature continued oblivious to the dramas and concerns of humans.

Then finally they were back at the villa, both of them turning their phones back on.

'How did they find out?' Chloe asked.

Logan drummed one finger on his thigh. 'I'm not sure. I didn't think my marriage would generate interest. It's not as though I'm in the gossip pages at all. I mean, if it was Belle getting married, then…' His voice trailed off.

'You think Belle did this?' Chloe stared at him and then bit her lip. 'We told her no publicity.'

'Yes, but she believed the only reason for that was to protect her from reporters whilst she is meant to be resting. Maybe she decided she doesn't need that protection any more.'

Chloe closed her eyes. 'She is worried about the effect on the company because people are worried about her health.'

'What better way to get ahead of potential speculation and fall out than to say she's in Mauritius attending her grandson's wedding. Happy news, positive feel-good publicity. I can see why it would have seemed like a logical step.'

Logan picked up his phone, punched a button and, a short phone call later, he nodded. 'That was an advertising executive at Belle's and she confirmed what we thought—she's asked us if we can do some publicity after the honeymoon.'

Incipient panic began to take hold. 'But we can't do that.' Chloe tried to keep her voice

224 THEIR MAURITIUS WEDDING RUSE

from rising, trying to think this through. 'There *is* no honeymoon.'

She looked round the villa, at the place that had been so full of joy and laughter, as she took in the bed still dishevelled, the clothes dropped to the floor and the flowers... Suddenly, the whole scene seemed to mock her, seemed to take on a tinge of sordidness. Because it was all a lie.

A fact that she could no longer hide from, because the illusion had been made public and was now open to scrutiny and speculation. It was no longer a temporary private bubble but a lie laid bare. She tried to ground herself by staring out at the vista that had seemed so beautiful just hours before, but everything was overshadowed now, tinged with grey, an illusion crumbling to ashes.

'Here's one of the articles,' Logan said, handing her his phone.

Chloe scanned the article.

Catch of the century Logan Jamieson, an 'off the radar' billionaire and grandson of Belle Jamieson, CEO and matriarch of Belle's Cosmetics, has got married!

His super-secret, whirlwind romance has culminated in a romantic wedding in Mauritius attended by the Belle herself, which leads us all to hope and presuppose that the stories of her ill health have been exaggerated.

Given her appearance, that certainly seems to be the case though, as the eighty-three-year-old told me in a video interview, 'My dear, I use my own products, designed to make the very best of every year, whatever your age.'

It was wonderful to see her look so well, and not just her. As the photo shows, the bride and groom looked pretty damn gorgeous too.

And who is the bride, you may well ask? Chloe Edwards, a corporate lawyer, and that is all I know.

But watch this space for further news of the happy couple...

Chloe studied the photo. The way she was looking up at Logan, the expression on her face, made it clear she was a bride in love, and now new panic seemed to clutch her heart. She didn't remember looking at Logan quite like that, all wide-eyed and gooey, as if...as if she really did love him.

Oh, God. Please, no.

That couldn't have happened, surely? Surely not? Her face seemed to leach of all colour and she put out a hand to steady herself as her head spun.

'Chloe. What's wrong? I know this has got out of hand, but we can work it out, work out what to do.'

But there was no *we*. The only possible future they had was a professional one, where they would meet across a desk, and every time she saw him, every time they shook hands, a tiny bit of her would die inside.

The irony twisted. All this had happened while she'd been lying to Belle, to Marie, Celeste, weaving a web of deceit—but in truth she'd been lying to herself. Telling herself that she was in control of her emotions, that this was all about attraction, that the growing closeness was a danger she could control, that she was willing to pay the price.

And now she knew the price—the pain of a love that could never be. Chloe would never risk bringing hurt to Logan's life even if he wanted her love. Which he didn't. So she wouldn't burden him with this revelation, with her love, not when he had made it plain that love was not a commodity he traded in. Any more than she did.

But she had brought hurt to someone else's life. Once again, it wasn't only herself who would have to pay. So would her mother. The future looked truly bleak, with no silver lining in sight, as the further ramifications hit her.

'There is nothing we can do to fix this,' she said. 'The world believes we are married; it's in the public domain. When we end this in a few weeks, there will be rife speculation. Someone will work out we lied, and that is going to impact on me professionally. Or people will believe I did it to further my career, to win Belle and your business, and then you found out. None of my clients will trust me; the partners will go nuts.'

Years of toil down the drain, another nail in the coffin of her hopes of someday earning her mother's pride in her. Another consequence of a lie—a broken heart, a broken career. This had to stop; she wouldn't, *couldn't*, keep lying. Not to herself, not to anyone. Now she knew her true feelings for Logan, knew they had to be kept secret, she couldn't pretend any more. Couldn't pretend to love someone she had genuinely fallen in love with, whilst hiding the fact that it was no longer an act for her. The idea of it was impossible. She had to walk away and face what she'd done. Alone.

Logan saw the shadows in her eyes, heard the flat despair in her voice and noted the arm around her midriff, as if to protect herself. All he wanted to do was take her in his arms and hold her, tell her it would all be all right. But he couldn't, sensing that she would reject any attempt to touch her, and that knowledge sent a wave of panic through him.

He had to work out how to fix this. Perhaps he should have seen this coming, or at least considered the risk, but he hadn't given it a thought, because he'd been so caught up in Chloe. Right from the start. Now he'd messed up and that was on him. He'd stepped onto the roller-coaster thinking he could control its journey—turned out he couldn't, and now they were plummeting. Somehow, he at least had to work out how to divert the journey to an upward trajectory. 'We can fix it,' he said, trying to imbue his voice with confidence, his brain processing ideas and risk analysis.

'How?'

Logan paced the cream marble floor, searching for a solution that felt just within his grasp. 'I've got it. We stay married.'

'Huh?' Chloe stared at him, shock in her hazel eyes—shock and an unidentifiable emotion, the green specks in her eyes bright.

'Why not?' The idea gathered steam. 'We can stay married for…as long as it suits us. Then when we break up it won't look strange. No one, including your work, need know we ever faked the marriage.'

That would work, surely? He watched her, her face unreadable as she looked out into the distance. She realised his heart was pounding against his rib cage and that he stood on the balls of his feet as he awaited her verdict. And it did feel like a verdict, one that mattered—mattered more than it should. Because with a bone-deep intensity he wanted Chloe to agree. He wanted more time with her, to wake up with her next to him, her head on his chest, or spooned in his arms; he wanted to walk hand in hand and see her smile, hear her laugh.

And now, seeing how still she stood, her face pale and set with no sign of relief, no hint of a smile, foreboding touched him. He felt fear, a foreknowledge that she wasn't going to agree, and that he was going to lose her, as he knew he must eventually. But not now. Not yet. Trying to keep his voice even, he forced himself to ask, 'What do you think? Pretty genius, right?'

Right? Please let it be right.

There was silence, then, 'We can't do that.'

'Why not?'

'Because all we are doing is propagating a lie, kicking the can down the road, and that will hurt more people.'

'I don't understand.'

'We can't keep lying to Belle. I can't get closer to her, keep giving her advice when I know at some point we are *going* to split up. We both know that she is hoping for a great-grandchild; she'll be watching, waiting, hoping. And it's not only her. It was my mum on the phone earlier, asking if it was true.'

Her voice was flat. 'You said to me that maybe I should work out another way to connect to my mother. Well, there is a way. She was furious and devastated when I broke up with Mike because she had hoped I'd marry him and have a baby. A son. A little boy I could name after my brother. A baby for her to love.'

Her voice broke. 'I even considered changing my mind, going back to Mike. But it wouldn't have been fair to him. Or to that potential baby. It would have been wrong. But now my mum believes we are a "happy couple", that this is the real thing, and she is already hoping, planning, happy…and I am going to have to dash that happiness. I can't let her keep believing for months. It's wrong.'

Logan absorbed her words and his heart twisted in his chest as so much became clear: at how profoundly complicated becoming a mother would feel for her; why Chloe was on the run from relationships. How could she make anything work with all that pressure, her mother's hopes weighing her down, the knowledge that her child would be seen as a replacement for her brother? The complications were rife and he couldn't blame her for deciding to eschew them.

'What your mother wants from you is neither right nor fair,' he said gently. 'You can't have a child for her. But equally you shouldn't give up the idea of having a child.'

Chloe took a deep breath. 'That is not what is in question now. The point is we can't keep living a lie. There have been too many lies and too many consequences.'

Shadows flitted across her eyes and Logan could feel her pain and how deep it went. 'We did this for Belle, but now the web we've woven has become too tangled, has trapped too many people, and no matter what we do people will get hurt. All we can do is minimise that hurt. But we cannot stay married; I cannot keep living a lie. We have to set things straight, restore our boundaries, focus on what is important.'

The words caught at him, each one like a sucker punch. Wasn't he, wasn't this, weren't *they* important? Everything they'd shared, everything they'd been to each other? But then he realised—no, it wasn't important. How could a few days in time be more important to Chloe than the principles she lived by? And now because she—because they—had lied, she stood to lose so much: the career she'd worked so hard for, her brother's dream and her mother's good opinion.

'What do you want to do?' he asked softly.

'We don't need to tell everyone the truth until after Belle's operation. I won't jeopardise Belle in any way, but we will need to say I got called away, back to London. A family or work emergency, or to get things ready for Belle—whatever excuse works. But Belle is the priority.'

Logan managed a nod. Of course he would be there for his grandmother. But he knew that knowledge would do nothing to alleviate the chasm that seemed to have opened in his chest, the bleak area of desolation that he couldn't make sense of. He'd had relationships that had lasted months and when it had been time to part he'd felt no more than a mild regret, if that. Nothing compared to this.

He couldn't bear the thought that he wouldn't hold her again, wouldn't see her face light up or see the hazel eyes speckle or fleck with laughter, passion or the first glimmers of waking in the morning. Would never again feel her head on his chest, the strawberry-blonde tendrils tickle his chest... And now pain sucker-punched him, even as he forced himself to stay still, to keep his face neutral. He would not show his hurt; he knew that to do so would hurt Chloe. She would feel it was a repeat of Mike and he wouldn't do that to her.

This whole charade had caused enough

pain and she'd made it clear that whatever had been between them was over. A wild longing soared to try to change her mind, to persuade her that his plan was best. But he couldn't do that.

Because it wasn't. It was Logan who had persuaded her to set aside her principles in the first place, convinced her that she should pretend to be his fiancée, and look where that had led. He couldn't ask her to set aside those principles and lie again. Not when it would hurt Belle, hurt her mother, hurt Chloe herself.

And he had so little to offer her. He couldn't risk love, or commitment; that path to happiness was not one he could tread.

'Logan?' Her voice was quiet and it seemed to him that it held so many questions. 'What do you think?'

The best, the only, thing he could do for Chloe now was play this the way she wanted to and show that he supported and respected her principles and her decisions. He had blithely said just days before that boundaries could be restructured, redrawn, and now he would have to do exactly that.

'I think you're right. It is time to stop, to set

things straight. I'll arrange a flight to London for you.' He took a deep breath.

He couldn't let her go without saying something, one last personal thing. 'These last days...they have been truly precious. Thank you for everything, for being you. For helping.'

Now she moved over to him and he could see the shadows in her eyes, and knew they weren't over him, but because of all she'd now lost because of him. She reached up and touched his cheek, the touch so gentle, so poignant and so unbearable at knowing that it would be the last time he felt her touch. And then slowly, with finality, she slipped the wedding and engagement rings from her finger, placed them on the table and walked away.

CHAPTER FIFTEEN

Three days later

CHLOE STARED AT her reflection and told herself that she could do this. Every instinct told her it was the right thing to do; she just hoped and prayed that it truly was. Last minute doubts assailed her: was this wrong, selfish, appalling? All she wanted to do was call Logan for reassurance, but she wouldn't. She knew Logan would be caught up with Belle, as he should be. And anyway, this was her life, and these were her decisions to make.

Though she knew that her time with him—confiding in him, the way he'd made her feel—had all contributed to this decision. In Mauritius with Logan she'd been herself—she'd been the Chloe who'd danced, who'd lost her inhibitions, who'd laughed, smiled and felt happy. And Logan had brought out that Chloe. He had *seen* her, listened to her and questioned some of the tenets she'd lived her life by for ten years.

Perhaps most of all he'd shown her that she was capable of love, that maybe there was nothing inherently wrong inside her and that she didn't have to bring misery wherever she went. Chloe knew she would always have to live with what had happened to her father and brother. But talking to Logan and hearing his story had made her see the possibility that, whilst what she had done had been wrong, she herself was not responsible for a tragedy she could not have predicted. Had not wanted. That she too had suffered loss.

He had shown her that she had a right to her own hopes and dreams. And, if she believed Logan's mother would have wanted him to live his dreams, maybe her dad and brother would have wanted Chloe to live hers. That she was more than just an unworthy substitute for her brother. But for the past ten years that was all she had been to her mother.

She raised her hand and rang the doorbell, waiting until her mother answered the door, her face pursed into the familiar line of disapproval.

'Come in.'

238 THEIR MAURITIUS WEDDING RUSE

Chloe followed her mother into the living room, still the same as it had been ten years ago—the carpet a little threadbare now, the curtains faded. There were photos everywhere of her dad and mum at their wedding, baby pictures of James, childhood snaps, his graduation dotted everywhere. And not a single picture of Chloe. Any stranger coming in wouldn't even know of her existence.

'You've got bad news.'

'I have news,' Chloe said, trying to have and to hold the courage she needed and to push down the guilt. 'I... I've resigned from my job. I realised that, whilst I do enjoy the law, and I don't regret becoming a lawyer at all, I don't want to be a corporate lawyer. I want to do something different with my skills. I want to help people, to make a difference.'

'Fair enough.' Her mother's tone was almost dismissive. 'Now that you've married, especially married money, you can afford not to work and focus on having a family.'

'It isn't that straightforward,' Chloe said, meeting her mother's eye. She couldn't tell her mother the full truth, not yet, not now— not until after Belle's operation in two days— but she could tell her *some* truth.

'Logan and I may not want to have children. Now or ever. I don't know what I want, but I do know that I can't have a child to replace James for you. It wouldn't be fair to anyone.'

Chloe forced herself to continue, needing to say everything she had to say before allowing her mother to speak. 'I am so sorry, Mum; so sorry for what happened to Dad and to James, and I wish with all my heart that I could turn time back and change what happened. But I never meant it to happen. All I did was sneak out to go to a party, just like I know James did in his time, just like so many of my friends did. I didn't want them to die. I loved them too,' she said, her voice low, tears pricking her eyes. Instead of blinking them back, she let them flow.

Her mother sat there, immobile, as Chloe continued.

'I love you too, Mum. And I wish, I wish, you could find it in yourself to forgive me. And if there is anything else I can do, any way I can make you proud of me, any way we can have a relationship, I would love that. I am so sorry; sorry for what you lost.'

She dug into her bag and pulled out a photo, one of the four of them smiling at the camera—her parents with their arms round each other, James and Chloe standing in front. Chloe carefully placed it on a table, walked over to her mum and put her arms around her resistant body. 'I'll call you tomorrow.'

With that she left, feeling a sense of freedom. She was no longer a corporate lawyer and she'd faced her mum with that decision. Her life was hers and she was free to dream.

But then, wasn't that what Logan had advised her to do—fulfil her own dreams? The idea was exhilarating and terrifying because part of doing that meant finding the courage to tell Logan the truth: that she loved him. After all her protestations about principle, she owed him that—more than that, she wanted him to know he was loved.

She had told him he deserved happiness, because he did, and she hoped that maybe he could take the risk of finding it with her. And, if he couldn't, then she would have to deal with it. But, no matter what she knew, she could never regret feeling this. Not any more.

The day before the operation

Logan stood staring out of the window, striving to keep his mind solely focused on Belle, but try as he might images of Chloe still surfaced. The ache of missing her was more than he could have imagined, the memories of their time together impossible to filter out. Even if he tried, she haunted his dreams.

The ring of his phone was a welcome diversion, the foolish leap of hope that it was Chloe was not.

But it wasn't. It was his dad.

Logan snatched up the phone. 'Dad?' he said. 'Thank God you've called.'

'Sounds a bit dramatic. What's going on? A reporter friend of mine contacted me, said I should contact you.'

Terrified his dad would get cut off, Logan kept it brief. 'Belle had a heart attack. She has a heart condition. She is having a massive operation tomorrow. Where are you? If you let me know the flight you'll be on, I'll get you from the airport.'

There was silence. 'Actually, Logan, I can't see the point of me jumping on a plane.'

Logan tried to process the words, disbelief superseding a sudden burn of rage. 'Well, let me help. The point is that you'll get a chance to see her before the operation. If anything goes wrong…'

'My being there won't change that. If something goes wrong, there will be nothing I can do for her. Right now I'm in a good place, and I don't want to unsettle that. I don't want to risk rocking the boat with emotional upset.'

'What if she dies?' He could barely bring himself to say it, but somehow he had to get his dad to see what was at stake here.

'Then there will still be nothing I can do. If she lives, there is no point in me coming.'

'So what exactly is the point for you?' Logan asked. 'Is there any *point* to having a family—a mother, a son?'

'Your mother never even got a chance to be a parent,' Matt said flatly. 'As for Belle, I am not sure she was ever much of a mother.'

'And me? Was I ever much of a son?'

There was silence, silence that spoke volumes, and something seismic shifted in Logan as Chloe's words echoed in his head: *Your father chooses to place blame where there is none.*

Logan didn't know the details of his father's childhood, but he did know the details of his own. He did know Belle and how she had brought him up. And he did know himself—he recalled all the times he had desperately tried to be a good son, reaching out to his father, hoping for forgiveness. But forgiveness for what? It *wasn't* his fault he had been born, and he did wish—wished oh, so very much—that his mother had lived. But maybe he had not been to blame for her death any more than Chloe had been to blame for her father's and brother's deaths.

'So you're definitely not coming,' he said now.

'No. I've thought about it and—'

'Thought about it. In the last three minutes?' And then the penny dropped. 'You got all my messages, didn't you? You've just been avoiding this, avoiding talking to me. Because you don't want the hassle, the emotions, that come with family, with caring.'

There was more silence, then, 'I guess you're right, Logan. I've got my life on an even keel. I like it that way. Tell Belle good luck from me.'

Logan hung up the phone and felt a sudden wave of sadness, a bleak realisation as he thought back to his dad's words and the fact that he was unwilling to come and see his mother for what could be the last time. Instead Matt put himself first, valuing his own

244 THEIR MAURITIUS WEDDING RUSE

happiness above others, with no thought as to what Belle might want, how she might be feeling, with no thought for Logan.

And Logan was no better than his father. He had taken on, trumpeted, endorsed the same life tenets and principles. He wouldn't take the risk of involvement, of love, of happiness.

There was Chloe's voice again, telling him his dad was...*affecting the decisions you are making. You don't owe him your happiness.*

What would bring him happiness? Or perhaps it was better to ask the question, *who* had brought him happiness over the past days? The answer was breathtaking in its simplicity: Chloe had. But he hadn't brought happiness to her; all he had done was talk about risks, investments and relationship withdrawal. Tangled her in a web of deceit that had brought her hurt and misery.

His thoughts were interrupted by a knock on the door that heralded Belle's nurse, Hilda.

'Your grandmother would like to see you.'

'Of course.' Resolutely Logan tried to banish the emotions that swirled inside him. This was the day before Belle's operation. Nothing mattered apart from her. He entered the living room and paused on the threshold. Belle sat propped up by cushions on the sofa and next to her was a man he recognised from the photo: Bertrand.

The older man rose to his feet and stepped forward, a still-youthful figure, smart in a blazer and chinos. He held out his hand. 'Bertrand Escalier. And you are Logan.'

'Yes. Good to meet you.' The two men shook hands and then Bertrand returned to Belle and sat down beside her as Logan took an arm chair.

'We've got something to tell you,' Belle said. 'About Bertrand.' A pause. 'And me. We're going to give it another try.'

'I...' Logan realised he had no idea what to say, no idea whether this was a good thing or a terrible one. He wished Chloe were here.

Bertrand took over. 'It's okay,' he said. 'I know you must have reservations. But Belle and I... From the moment I saw her a few days ago, it was like when we first met...a bolt from the blue...and over the past few days we have talked and talked, said all the things I wish we had said all those years ago.'

Bertrand paused and looked at Belle, and Logan felt a sudden sense of wonder at the look they exchanged. He could see love, and

246   THEIR MAURITIUS WEDDING RUSE

the awe it inspired, shine. 'Your grandmother and I…we are meant to be.'

Belle nodded. 'I wish…we had tried harder years ago. I wish I hadn't walked away. Or, once I had, I wish I'd walked back, swallowed my pride and my fears. You see, Logan, I was scared. Scared I'd be hurt again, and so I didn't go back, didn't try.'

'And I, too, was scared. Scared of rejection, scared of hurt…'

Belle raised a hand. 'Don't get us wrong. Both Bertrand and I have lived long, fulfilled, happy lives. But when we saw each other again, when we realised how…right this feels, neither of us wanted to walk away again. To walk away from a second chance.' She looked up at Logan. 'I would like to know I have your blessing.'

Now Logan smiled. He could see the hope, the love and the joy that surrounded them. What kind of person would deny them this or cast doubts in the way of that? 'You have it,' he said. 'I am truly happy for you both.'

Belle looked at him quizzically. 'No risk assessment?' she asked. 'No advice on investing time and risking hurt?' Her smile widened. 'Chloe has changed you.'

Logan absorbed the words and felt them impact and race round his brain, his whole being, as he acknowledged the truth of them. Chloe had changed him—made him see the world differently, see himself differently. Made him see that maybe he did deserve happiness and that love was worth the risk. Yes, perhaps it could bring hurt, but it could also bring joy. To deny love, avoid risk, eschew involvement, as his father had done, made his life less, made it muted, made it smaller.

'Yes, she has,' he said simply. 'For the better.'

'Then don't make the mistakes we made,' Belle said. 'I don't know what's going on between you—I don't know why you got married—but I do know that, if you love her, you shouldn't walk away.' She looked closely at him. 'And believe in yourself. Don't believe that you can't make her happy. Give yourself, give Chloe, give love, a chance.'

'Your grandmother is right,' Bertrand said. 'If your Chloe is worth fighting for, then fight. Don't walk away because you are scared of hurt. Or scared full-stop. Because if you do you may regret it for the rest of your life.'

A tsunami of emotion cascaded through Logan at the knowledge that he loved Chloe.

248 THEIR MAURITIUS WEDDING RUSE

At the sense of exultation and sense of fear, that admitting that love—a desire to tell Chloe and let her know that she was loved, cared about and appreciated—would be rejected.

Walking over to the couple on the sofa, he leant down and embraced Belle in a hug that he hoped expressed the love he had for her and his appreciation for all she'd done for him. Then he offered a handshake and a smile for Bertrand, which he hoped expressed his approval.

'Thank you both,' he said. He vowed he would go to Chloe after the operation, once he knew that Belle was alright, as surely she would be now. Because when he went to Chloe he wanted it to be when she knew he was focused completely on her. Anticipation, hope and love filled his heart.

Chloe approached the hospital, not sure if this was the right thing to do or not, but also knowing she couldn't leave Logan to wait there on his own. during the interminable hours waiting to see if Belle would make it. She pushed open the waiting-room door and paused on the threshold, trying to gather herself together and somehow keep the love that she couldn't control show on her face, in her eyes and in her voice. It wasn't fair to tell Logan now, not until after the operation; not until they knew Belle was going to make it.

This time now was all about Belle.

As she entered Logan turned and for an instant his face seemed to light up as he looked at her. Then he rose and blinked, as if to shut the expression down, though his smile remained.

'How is she? I hope it's okay that I'm here.' Nerves strummed along with worry that he didn't want her here and that she shouldn't have come. 'I can wait somewhere else if you like.'

'No.' The syllable was instant, urgent even. 'Stay. Please. I'm glad you're here. There's no news yet, but she was in great spirits when she went in.'

'I spoke to her this morning, to wish her luck.'

He nodded and now she could see the strain on his face. She could only imagine how scared he was. 'She told me about Bertrand—said she had so much to live for, that she knew she'd be seeing me soon.'

'I told Bertrand to go and rest. He's booked

into a hotel nearby. I promised to call as soon as we hear anything.'

'Do you like him?'

'Yes, I do. I'm happy for them, happy they are giving themselves a chance.'

Chloe glanced at him sideways, saw that he meant it and suddenly a tendril of hope surfaced in her heart.

They sat in silence after that, close but without touching, both thinking of Belle. Chloe hoped her presence gave him some comfort and believed it did, when at one point during the wait she realised he had taken her hand in his.

Then finally a doctor entered, her face tired but smiling as they both jumped to their feet, still hand in hand.

'It was a success. Belle is an amazing woman and we are confident she will be okay. She is still under the anaesthetic, but when she comes round you can see her for a short time.'

Logan rocked back on his heels as Chloe exhaled a sigh of relief.

'Thank you,' they both said together, and the doctor smiled and turned to go.

Once the door had swung shut, Chloe turned to Logan. 'I am so glad.' Tears of happiness welled as she smiled at him, knowing what a weight must have lifted from him. 'I'll go now. But give her my love. Tell her I'll come and see her tomorrow.'

'Wait. Please don't go. I... I need to talk to you. I just need to call Bertrand first.'

Chloe halted, trying not to let hope take over even as her heart beat a little quicker. 'Of course.'

She waited whilst he passed on the good news then turned back to her. 'He sounded relieved and happy and full of plans for the future.' Logan took a deep breath. 'Which is why I asked you to wait.'

'To discuss Bertrand and Belle?' Disappointment doused the glimmer of hope.

'No. To discuss... Well, I wanted to tell you... I mean, well, actually I wasn't going to tell you anything, I was going to wait,' he continued. 'In fact, I had a plan. But I can't wait. It's too important. So I guess...'

Chloe stared at the usually assured Logan Jamieson and it dawned on her: Logan was nervous. And part of her panicked, terrified he had something bad to tell her.

'What is it? Is anything wrong?'

'No. Or at least, I don't think so. I mean, I don't know. I don't want to...' He stopped.

252 THEIR MAURITIUS WEDDING RUSE

'Sorry. I don't know what's wrong with me. I've never done this before and it's scary, because I don't want to upset you. I don't want you to feel like this is a repeat of Mike. I... Damn it... I love you.'

Now he smiled, a tentative smile but a smile nonetheless as he repeated the words. 'I love you. It's okay. I am not expecting you to love me back, but I wanted you to know. And I am hoping you'll give me, give us, a chance to build on what we already have. I know it may take time, and we can take it as slow as you want. We'll play by your rules. If...if it's what you want, but I hope it is.'

It occurred to Chloe that she needed to say something, that she stood rooted to the spot, filled with so many joyful emotions that she was rendered speechless with sheer happiness. But she needed to tell Logan the truth.

'It's okay. There are no rules. Because I... I love you too, Logan. I love you with all my heart.'

'You love me?' He looked dazed.

'Yes. I love you, Logan Jamieson. I love you for your kindness, the way you listen to me, the way you make me laugh. I love you because you saw the real me. You made me see who I am and that I am not responsible for my father's and brother's deaths. You made me see that it is okay to have my own dreams, my own life. I quit my job. I told my mother that I love her, that I want to be part of her life but I couldn't live a lie any more.

'You enabled me to make that decision. And most of all you made me see I am capable of love. Because I love you with all my heart. So, yes, I do want to build on everything we have. I want to grow with you, learn with you, support you through the highs and the lows. As long as that is definitely what you want—if you're sure?'

'I am sure. I know what I said about not wanting commitment or love or emotions, not wanting the highs and lows. I was wrong— wrong to believe that love isn't worth the risk of loss. Loving you, being with you, is worth any risk. You've made me see that I don't have to be like my father, that I am not him. That I don't have to live a life without love or happiness.

'You see, I did think that somehow it wasn't fair if I found happiness; that somehow I had to balance out my parents' loss. You showed me that isn't true. I can pursue happiness, my dreams... I can love and be loved. I've decided that I will take on Belle's Cosmetics, learn the ropes and allow Belle to take a back step, retire or semi-retire if she wants to with Bertrand.'

'I'm so glad.' And she was. She knew that Logan would love and thrive with the challenge, and Belle would be overjoyed that her company would pass to safe hands. 'And I will help in any way I can.'

'Just as I'll help you take up any new challenge, any new career path, you decide to take—be it environmental law, humans rights, retraining as a teacher... Whatever you decide, I'll be there by your side. I want to wake up with you every day; I want to explore the possibility of a family if that's what you want.'

Chloe blinked back a tear as a sudden picture crossed her mind of she and Logan: Logan holding the hand of a little girl with blonde curls; she holding a spiky-haired, blond baby boy.

'I love you,' she said as he put his hand in his pocket and went down on one knee, there in the hospital waiting room.

Logan took out two rings: the rose-gold

wedding band and the engagement ring she'd returned to him days before.

'Chloe Edwards, will you agree to do me the honour of staying married to me for the rest of our lives? To ride the roller-coaster with me, for better or worse, in sickness and in health, and to go through the ups and downs together for ever?'

'I do. I do agree with all my heart.'

And in that moment Chloe knew that she and Logan would truly be happy riding that roller-coaster for life. Together. Happy to hold the responsibility of giving and receiving love. For ever.

* * * * *

*If you enjoyed this story,
check out these other great reads
from Nina Milne*

Cinderella's Moroccan Midnight Kiss
Bound by Their Royal Baby
His Princess on Paper
Snowbound Reunion in Japan

All available now!

Harlequin® Reader Service

Enjoyed your book?

Try the perfect subscription for Romance readers and get more great books like this delivered right to your door.

See why over 10+ million readers have tried Harlequin Reader Service.

Start with a Free Welcome Collection with free books and a gift—valued over $20.

Choose any series in print or ebook.
See website for details and order today:

TryReaderService.com/subscriptions